Praise

"James creates powerful intimacy and terror…a seriously creepy page-turner that will keep readers up all night."

—Publisher's Weekly on *Q Island*

"James has a talent for combining action-packed vignettes into a powerful, fast-paced whole."

—Library Journal on Black Magic

"…made me wish for a sequel. I'd recommend Blood Red Roses to anyone looking for something dark yet intelligent. It kept me on my toes from beginning to end!"

—Long and Short Reviews on *Blood Red Roses*

(Five Stars, A Night Owl Top Pick) "I loved the story so much that I'm eagerly waiting to read more from him. He carefully and very intricately wove his storyline to have elements of mystery and suspense throughout. I now have a new favorite book I'll read over and over again."

—Night Owl Reviews on *Dark Inspiration*

"The book had me at the edge of my seat. The writing is so vivid I even jumped a few times. If you're a fan of the genre, love ghosts and are drawn to the supernatural, then do yourself a favor and pick up a copy of this book!"

—Long and Short Reviews on *Dark Inspiration*

This was a wonderful tale that had me drawn in from the beginning, fascinated by the vividness of the storytelling. While there's plenty of the somewhat gruesome and occult we horror fans love so much, it's the depth and emotions of the characters that truly make this a fabulous read.

—The Entertainer Magazine on *Dark Vengeance*

Also by Russell James

<u>Novels</u>
Dark Inspiration
Sacrifice
Black Magic
Dark Vengeance
Dreamwalker
Q Island

<u>Novellas</u>
Blood Red Roses

<u>Collections</u>
Out of Time
In a Land Far Away…
Tales from Beyond
Deeper into Darkness
Still Out of Time
Forever Out of Time

OUTER RIM

**Six Stories
from the
Galaxy's Edge**

RUSSELL JAMES

Russell James

Outer Rim

Six Stories from the Galaxy's Edge

Print Version

All stories copyright 2014 by Russell James.

ISBN-13: 978-1537196589

ISBN-10: 1537196588

MLG Publishing
Longwood, FL 32779

For Paul, Teresa, Belinda, and Janet,
all residents of the Final Frontier.

Contents

Ars Gratia Artis

Mishell entered the kitchen wearing her favorite outfit, the green dress with white swirls that blended into stripe along its short hemline.

Her father looked up from the table and sighed.

"Mish, you really ought to wear something more mainstream. The Level Out ceremony vidcast goes everywhere. It's your first impression at your new assignment."

"Where I'm going, this'll make the perfect impression."

Her father slid aside his chipped bowl of runny oatmeal. It clinked his cup and sent the oily sheen in his cold coffee into a swirl. A permanent stain of brown tar splotched the left sleeve of his starched sanitation coveralls. He took a deep breath, like a mountain climber before assailing a steep face.

"Look, I've been telling you all year, the odds of you going to Artisia Colony are thousands to one. You can't get your hopes up so high."

Mishell swept her long blonde hair behind her shoulders. Her blue eyes sparkled like the Caribbean Sea did a hundred years ago. She bounced on her toes with anticipation. Her father's face sagged.

"I have the best grades in my class, in any graduating class. My drawings won three awards this year. I haven't missed a day of school since primary phase, never even been late. No one better qualifies for Artisia Colony."

"And you also qualify for any of the top low orbit stations, like the Wellian Science Academy, or Design Station Regula. Only one transport a month goes to Venus and Artisia Colony. Then, only a few on each transport are fresh graduates."

The cloistered residents of Artisia Colony sent back all the art, all the literature, all the music the overcrowded residents of Earth consumed. The artists wanted for nothing, freed to pursue their creative passions.

Her father stood and approached her. He placed a calloused hand on her shoulder. "Mish, three-quarters of your class won't even leave Earth. They'll have to make the best of it. If you get an off-world assignment, any assignment, you should be grateful."

Mishell pushed herself away. Her face flushed red.

"You just don't want me to go to Artisia because that's where Mother went. Because she took her opportunity and left you here."

Fury flashed in her father's eyes. "Don't forget that she left you here as well. One month old with a neonatal tranx addiction from her abuse. That was her parting gift to you."

"Her art was so good, she was reassigned to Artisia years after graduation, reassigned out of sanitation." She brushed a finger across his coverall in contempt. "Of course she'd leave. She'd have taken me if she'd been permitted."

Her father slammed a hand on the table hard. Coffee slopped out of his cup.

"Wake up from your fantasy, girl! It's time you knew the tough truth. She had no such thoughts. They offered Artisia, and she jumped. She knew the colony was sequestered, she knew she'd never communicate with anyone off-station again, except through her art. She didn't care. She threw some clothes in a plastic bag, and was out the door to Central Transport within the hour."

Mishell recoiled at this new version of her mother's departure. "I don't believe you. You're…you're making that up to make me stay close to you. Well, it's not going to happen. I'm not going to stay here, another cog in the mindless machine that keeps humanity's head above water."

She marched to the apartment door, pulled it open, and looked back over her shoulder.

"Don't even come to Level Out. I don't want your disappointment to bring me down when they announce I'm going to Artisia."

Sadness washed the anger from her father's face. Mishell smirked with triumph and slammed the door behind her.

◆◆◆

The Level Out had become one of the city's great events. Tens of thousands filled the AthletiDome, hundreds of strangers for every family member of a graduate. The graduates' records were public knowledge, as were their Selections, the three wishes they had for their assignment. Bets small and large rode on some outcomes. People had their own favorites, often championed by the media.

Bright lights lit the stage and the line of Level Out grads. Camera drones zoomed about like gnats, each linked to the vidstream millions were tuned to.

One by one, each graduate mounted the stage in the end zone and stood before the Chancellor, the black-robed master who held their fate in his hands. A perfect silence preceded the Chancellor's confirmation of each student's Level Out, and his reveal of the grad's assignment.

Then, an explosion of emotion filled the stadium. Cheers for the ones who went sub-orbital, laughter for the disappointed majority who remained Earth-bound, and jeers for the haughty and despised when they drew a deserved, lowly status.

Mishell stood in the line of graduates. The great snake moved ahead two steps, and paused, two steps, and paused. Names and assignments boomed out across the AthletiDome, followed by wild responses. She barely heard any of it. She wiped her sweating palm against her dress. Her pounding heart thundered in her ears. In seconds, she'd hear her name, and then the two most beautiful words in the world. Artisia Colony. All she'd worked for, all she'd dreamed about would finally happen. She'd kick the dust of this filthy, crowded planet from her feet, stop being the daughter of a sanitation worker, and become the daughter, and protégé, of a great artist.

Her turn came. She stepped to the edge of the stage. The Chancellor stood meters away, the usual dour look on his face. An assistant in a black suit stood behind him, ready to usher each newly-minted citizen off stage, and keep the flow going.

The crowd hushed. Mishell smiled and strode across the platform. Her skirt swayed about her knees. Someone in the crowd whistled. Several people laughed. Hundreds shushed them.

"Mishell Arthur," the Chancellor said. "You Level Out with a perfect 4.0 average."

He handed Mishell her graduate ID card and shook her hand. He touched his earpiece. Mishell gripped her new ID so tightly she nearly cracked it.

When he spoke again, she barely heard him. He opened his mouth, and her mind filled in "Artisia Colony." But his lips weren't synced to her words. His voice bounced inside her head several times, the phrase too unbelievable to process, until it finally forced comprehension.

"Design Station Regula."

The crowd went wild. A wave of cheers greeted this news, an assignment the remaining graduates would sacrifice body parts to have. Mishell staggered one step forward, then looked back, confused.

A mistake. Surely, an oversight. Assignments must have been out of order. She'd ask the Chancellor to double check—

The assistant stepped up, whipped an arm around her waist, and practically flung her down the steps on the stage's far side. She tripped on the last step and collapsed on the playing field. Another name and another assignment thundered out across the Dome and sent the crowd crazy.

Design Station Regula. State housing projects. Business buildings. Public restrooms. Her artistic talent couldn't be wasted on such pedestrian pursuits. The idea of being trapped in sub-orbit, with this humanity-choked world still within sight, deciding what shade of tan to paint washroom walls, made her sick. That wasn't going to happen. It couldn't happen.

Graduates danced off the stage into the arms of excited, waiting parents. Mishell stood and swept the flecks of artificial turf from her legs. She stared daggers into the back of the Chancellor's head.

He wasn't going to keep her from Artisia Colony. Her father wasn't, either. And she'd die before she ever set foot on Design Station Regula.

◆◆◆

Three days later, and one day after the transport for Artisia Colony departed with great fanfare, she entered the sprawling terminal of Central Transport. Her scheduled shuttle to Design Station Regula launched from the East Pads. She walked west.

She shifted her travel bag higher on her shoulder. Brushes and palettes filled the lower third. Artisia would have these things, of course, but these were her favorites, left behind by her mother. Her father said her mother abandoned them in her haste, but Mishell knew they were meant to be her legacy. How excited her mother would be to know that her daughter had learned to paint with the brushes she'd left for her.

The utilitarian west cargo pads looked nothing like the plush passenger wing opposite. Concrete floors, corrugated steel walls. The rumble of forklifts everywhere. The air smelled of spilled fuel and hot plastic.

Mishell entered the open door to Bay 9. The cargo vessel's captain, a scruffy looking man with three day's beard and a scarred nose, perused a tablet in his hands. He matched her contact's description perfectly. She walked up next to him.

"I'm Mishell Arthur."

"Yeah, I guessed that. Not many girls wander into cargo bays. Fair warning, my ship's not rated for passengers. We get boarded by Customs, they'll send you back home, best case scenario. You sure you want to do this?"

"I came to you, not the other way around. I'm ready." She pulled out the wad of credits she got from cashing in the shuttle ticket her father had bought her. She added her month's expense money and handed it to the captain. "When do we leave?"

"As soon as you get on board. Now, so we're clear, when I pick up cargo from Artisia Colony, I don't see anybody. They never break their isolation. I dock, I load up the paintings or statues or whatever from the cargo bay, sign a manifest, and I leave. All I'm doing is leaving you behind. I'm not introducing you to the colony or anything. When they find you, I'll swear you stowed away and I've never seen you. You're on your own, kid."

"I get it."

But she wasn't going to be on her own at all. She'd be with family.

◆◆◆

Mishell's cargo vessel passed the Artisia transport on its way back from Venus. The disembarked passengers would have a day's start on her when she got there. They would have sent their final message home from the transport to confirm their arrival. They would have just started to integrate into the wonderful community of generations of Earth's finest artists. Mishell wasn't fazed. With her mother's help, she'd catch up quick, and then pull way ahead.

◆◆◆

Artisia Colony's cargo bay doors closed, and left Mishell in complete silence. The cargo bay seemed three times its initial size with the horde of statues, paintings, tapestries, and other amazing artwork now aboard her departing cargo ship. She waited in a corner, assuming a colonist would enter to check the empty bay. But no one did. She shrugged her shoulders and decided to make the first move.

She stepped over to the pressure door that opened to the rest of the station. She fluffed her hair with her fingers. A quick tug aligned the hem of her short green dress, finally worn for the right occasion. The same nervous joy she felt ascending the steps to Level Out returned at double strength. Her hands quivered against the wheel that held the door shut. She imagined the colony's interior, decorated by the planet's greatest artists. She suppressed a giggle. Taking a deep, excited breath, she spun the wheel.

The door opened to a room the half the size of the cargo bay. An enormous 3D printer sat in the middle of the floor. Its four printer arms hung idle, pointing down as if sleeping. Workstations filled the rest of the room, workaday consoles like she'd seen in dozens of space craft and businesses. A large view screen at the far end of the room showed Venus' angelic, swirling white atmosphere.

Two strong arms grabbed her from behind and whirled her around. A burly man in a Stellar Fleet lieutenant's uniform gave her a violent shake.

"Who the hell are you and what are you doing here?"

"I was…late. I missed the transport."

"No you didn't. Everyone who was assigned here arrived yesterday. You weren't on the manifest."

A thin brunette with a severe haircut entered from the other side. She wore a Stellar Fleet captain's uniform.

"Lieutenant, what the…whoa, who the hell is this?"

"No clue, Cap."

Mishell writhed in the man's arms. This was going all wrong. Mishell knew she had to get past these guards, into the colony proper. She went still, and played her trump card.

"I'm Mishell Arthur, my mother, Harmony Arthur, is here on the colony. I'm an artist, here to join her."

That would get her through. She set her jaw.

14

The captain approached. An icy smile crossed her face. She bent down so her eyes met Mishell's.

"And when did your mommy arrive here, little girl?"

Mishell's hands turned to fists at the woman's infuriating, condescending tone.

"Eighteen years ago."

"Ah, well you missed her. She stepped out."

"I demand you take me into the colony!"

"Well, if you demand it..." the woman said.

The lieutenant released her. The captain took both of Mishell's hands in hers, and pulled her one step forward. "Ta da! Welcome to Artisia!"

The two fleet officers burst into laughter.

"No, not here," Mishell said. "With the artists…where are they?"

"Who needs artists?' the captain said. She pointed to a workstation beside the printer. "Our database contains every piece of art ever created. Every drawing, every book, every poem. The world's already created so much art, that mankind has forgotten ninety-nine percent of it. Why make new art when we can just re-print something old? It's all new to the masses, anyway."

"The best and the brightest," Mishell said, "they all came here. What do they do?"

The two officers laughed again.

"Seriously," the lieutenant said. "This never gets old. The look on their faces is priceless."

"We don't get the best of anything here," the captain said. "We get the worst. Flakes that can't generate enough value to feed themselves. The non-productive, the head-in-the-clouds dreamers who think that writing a novel or carving a picture frame makes the world a better place. Making ball bearings is what makes the world a better place."

Something thudded against the view screen. The splayed corpse of a young woman floated by. A first place sculpture award medal floated around her neck on a blue ribbon.

"So the Fleet says to space them when they get here," the captain said. "They float around the station for a few days before Venus pulls them in. It's really funny sometimes."

Thousands? Tens of thousands? she thought. How many shuttles full of artists had come here over the years? All of them dead, cremated in a fiery entry into toxic Venus? Including her mother, selected not because her talent was valued, but because it wasn't.

Tears welled in Mishell's eyes. She staggered back from the screen and bumped into one of the printer arms. The woman's smile disappeared.

"And, my dear, as an artist yourself, you'll have to join them."

A black cloud of dread enveloped Mishell. Her pulse raced.

"No, no," Mishell said. "I'll-I'll just go home. I won't tell anyone."

"All these supposedly creative people," the captain said, "all say the same thing."

"Wait," the lieutenant said. "I got a better idea."

Mishell's eyes went wide with anticipation. Hope for a reprieve soared.

The man opened a closet and rummaged around in a pile of clothes at the bottom. "I'm sick of cleaning this place. You know how many times I've scrubbed the toilets over the years? Let's keep her alive and have her take care of that."

The captain arched a brow and nodded in approval. The lieutenant pulled a piece of clothing from the pile and tossed it at Mishell. A pair of dirty coveralls landed at her feet. They stank of mold and urine.

"That pair ought to fit."

Ω

Sekhmet Rising

An Eddie Kane Adventure

Twelve crates of used reactor parts now sat in the Centauri Station customs holding area. *Electra's* cargo bay yawned empty. Captain Eddie Kane stood in the docking module between the two. Transporting used parts was one step above hauling garbage, but it was two steps above flying empty. He had under an hour before he had to clear space dock, under an hour to find a paying cargo.

His trademark brown mesh jacket covered the top half of his gray nanosuit. Tarnished fleet captain's bars clung to his jacket epaulets. And while he could still remember winning the jacket in a ritacaro game, he could not for the life of him remember where he'd purloined the officer's rank. He leaned back against the docking module and scratched at his black goatee. Allison walked up through *Electra's* cargo bay.

"Worried?' she asked.

"No, I'm just thinking."

"No, when you scratch at that scraggly facial hair, you *say* you're thinking, but you're really just worried." She tucked her short blonde hair behind one ear in that way Eddie always found irresistible.

"Are you saying I have a tell?"

"Please," she sighed. "Which of us always loses at Junian poker?"

"I thought that was because you cheated."

"Like I need to." Her smile vanished, replaced by the serious look that meant she'd mentally shifted roles from wife to ship's engineer. "I ran a diagnostic on the ion baffles, and then did a visual. They aren't going to re-align themselves, you know. We've got about a hundred hours before we're restricted to half speed."

Eddie caressed her cheek with his fingertips. "How can a face so beautiful deliver such bad news?"

"I'm serious, Eddie. What's your plan?"

"I'm working on it."

"That answer never turns out well."

Eddie levered himself up from the bulkhead so could exploit the two inches in height he had on his wife. He looked down into her

17

blue eyes. A lock of his dark hair fell down across his forehead. He was pretty sure she thought that was sexy.

"I'll make it work."

He hugged her. Some of the tension inside her relaxed.

"You'd better, Eddie."

"Please, crewman," he whispered in her ear, "call me captain."

"I can barely stand to call you husband," she whispered back. "Don't push it."

She walked back across *Electra's* vacant cargo bay. He followed the sway of her hips inside her skintight nanosuit, as he had every day since they met. If he did have to cross the galaxy at half speed with someone…

"Are you Kane?" came a deep voice from behind him.

Eddie spun around. A stout little man with an unflattering receding hairline and close set eyes stood in the customs area. He wore a dark suit with a red string tie that passed for business professional these days. He didn't have a customs pass around his neck.

"Should you be in here?" Eddie asked.

"In fifty minutes, you won't be," he said. "Do you want to leave empty?"

"Depends on what I'm hauling."

The man smiled with a set of crooked teeth. "A docking ring on the way out and riches on the way back."

He reached into his pocket, and pulled a dampening field generator from his pocket. He stuck the gray box's magnetized frame to the docking module bulkhead, and turned it on.

"Aren't those illegal?" Eddie said.

"Mildly. Like a lot of the cargo you run."

Whoever this guy was, he'd done his research.

"Name's Arno Proctor. I want to find the *Sekhmet*."

Eddie's heart skipped a beat. This guy *had* done his research.

The *Sekhmet* had been a warship rumored outfitted with every cutting edge technology, including conductive fluid power transmission and stealth tech. All the tactical systems were said to be controlled through holographic interface. Not just tiny console displays like *Electra* had, but fully immersive versions in place of any control panels at all. The ship's massive expense sunk the prospect of a fleet of sisters while it was still a paper plan.

The *Sekhmet* was designed for combat, but on its maiden voyage, she only carried diplomatic cargo, the Chalice of Yangor, a jeweled gold goblet returning to its home world. Everything Eddie read said that the *Sekhmet* had been ambushed by a horde of Black Shirt ships that made quick work of her escorts. She exhausted all munitions and was driven into a plasma cloud's asteroid field. She never came out, presumed pulverized. Presumed by everyone but Eddie, that is.

"Keep talking," Eddie said.

"The government of Yangor hired me to retrieve their missing chalice. Word is you might know where the ship is."

"How would you know that?" Eddie said.

"You talk a lot in bars. Of course it might be all talk."

The *Sekhmet* has been Eddie's hobby/obsession since its loss. He'd been enthralled by the compelling, tragic story of the Alliance flagship lost in combat with all aboard. In his free time, he'd combed the records of its final encounter, recalculated the positions of asteroids and moons, and plotted a probable drift course. He imagined finding her floating in space. He has a damn good idea where it was, but never the time or money to check out his hunch.

Eddie squared his shoulders. "I can get you to her. But it won't be cheap."

"As a down payment, I'll fully fuel your ship." Proctor then quoted a fee for payment on delivery that was twice what *Electra* was worth. "Interested?"

Eddie tried to mask his relief and enthusiasm. He reached out to shake Proctor's hand. "Deal."

The man's hand was cold, but his grip was like a hydroclamp. Proctor smiled again, all jumbled teeth and thin red lips. This time it made Eddie nervous.

"I've a custom docking ring that will mate with the *Sekhmet.* I'll get it installed."

Eddie has a dozen questions, but Proctor pulled the dampener from the wall and pocketed it. He returned to the station. Eddie wondered what he'd just gotten himself into.

Eddie returned to the *Electra's* wedge-shaped bridge. Wide viewports gave him a panoramic view of Centauri Station and the stretches of space beyond. The ship was designed for more of a crew than Eddie could ever pay. The comm and nav stations sat empty. Allison stood at engineering.

"Eddie, these gauges show we're fueling. How are we going to pay for—"

Something clanked against the hull. Allison stood and looked out the viewport. Her jaw dropped.

"What the hell? There are spacewalkers clamping something to Airlock 2."

"We have a contract," Eddie said. "Salvage work. The government of Yangor is sending us to find the *Sekhmet*. They want the sacred chalice back."

"What? When?"

"A few minutes ago."

The hull noise stopped and the station reeled the spacewalkers back in.

"Damn it, Eddie, when are you going stop jumping into things?"

"Look, we need to clear space dock in minutes. The whole thing came together fast."

A light flashed on the engineering board.

"Someone's sealing the cargo bay airlock," Allison said.

She pulled up the video link of the cargo bay. Proctor stood there with two enormous men. The twin muscleheads' broad shoulders stretched their dark nanosuits tight. They both sported bushy, dark Mohawks and the stereotypical proportions of the chemically enhanced; low, protruding foreheads, massive top-heavy bodies, tiny waists and tree trunk legs.

"They don't look remotely Yangorian." Allison said.

"Now that you mention it…" Eddie said.

They both went to the cargo bay. Proctor stood flanked by the two walking slabs of beef. Tattoos of braided thorns encircled their necks.

"Who are these two?" Eddie said.

"Roman and Sergei. Salvage crew. I don't do heavy lifting."

"It's a one-man job. The chalice isn't in a black hole."

"No," Proctor said. "You're convinced it's in the Epsilon 14 sector of the asteroid belt, right? So I'll worry about my associates, you worry about getting us there. Or we can defuel your little bucket of bolts here, and find someone else."

Eddie had worked his ass off to captain his own ship. He didn't like anyone berating *Electra*, and he absolutely hated someone else giving him orders. Allison wasn't any more forgiving. Behind him, he could practically feel the heat radiating off her as she wound up to give Proctor a round of hell.

But it was Proctor's fuel, and defueling would keep *Electra* in dock with a surcharge. And then he'd be adrift without cargo. And they needed this money. And trumping all those practical reasons to hold his tongue, he'd miss the chance to find the *Sekhmet*.

"Take seats in the galley," Eddie said. "We undock in minutes."

Proctor gave him a snaggle-toothed smile that Eddie was well into loathing. "See you on the bridge in six hours."

Eddie turned to see Allison's stunned look of incredulity. He passed her, and she followed him back to the bridge.

"What did you get us into?" she said. "Did you see the tattoos on those thugs' necks? They're enforcers for the Consortium."

Of course he recognized the brandings of the pervasive underworld organization. The Consortium served all the Alliance's vices. A visit from someone with a tattooed thorn necklace usually meant your will had better be in order.

"Well, obviously I didn't see those two until just now," Eddie said. He scratched his goatee. "Yangor, the Consortium, what difference does it make? The air lock weapons scanners didn't trigger, so they aren't armed. This'll work out. I know plenty of captains that have safely done a little work for the Consortium."

He really didn't.

♦♦♦

The targeting computer flashed that it had an active signal. Eddie practically jumped from his captain's chair. For the past six hours, he'd double checked his research, broken down the gravitational data by hand, studied the long range probe data. It all said he'd find her here. And sure as hell, there she was.

21

"Well," Allison sighed. She'd cooled down during the long passage. She tapped a command into the console at her navigation station. "I'll be damned if you weren't right."

"*Again*," Eddie corrected. "That's *right, again.*"

"Even you get a lucky day now and then." Allison smiled.

"That kind of disrespect is why I should never hire family."

He stroked his goatee as he studied the asteroid that filled the bridge's forward view port. It was as large as some of Saturn's smaller moons, a dusty, orange-tinged, cratered sphere. It registered as 78% iron, enough mass and metal to conceal the stealth-sheathed *Sekhmet* from all but short rage scans. Just as he'd predicted.

"Take the asteroid on the port side," Eddie said. "Slow to approach speed. No point in hitting her after we've come this far."

Allison turned from her station. Her blonde bangs framed blue eyes turned cold as a comet's core. Her smile was gone. "Eddie, seriously, this setup feels bad. This doesn't seem a little odd to you? This guy knows your obsession—"

Eddie raised a finger in protest at the characterization. Allison cut him off with a slash of her hand across her throat.

"Yes, obsession," she continued. "And then he knows *Electra* well enough have a custom-made docking clamp, and to correctly estimate our time to target?"

"This little trip will net us in one trip what we make in years of cargo runs."

"If they don't kill us afterwards. Look, you found the *Sekhmet*, just like you always said you could. I'll turn *Electra* about before we visually confirm it. We'll head home, say we couldn't find it, and live our lives in peace."

The idea had more merit than he wanted to admit. But a few hundred miles from his personal version of the lost city of Atlantis, he couldn't turn back.

"This'll be fine, Angel. In and out and paid before you know it."

Arno Proctor stepped onto the bridge. The pudgy man hadn't taken to space travel at all. Bloodshot eyes and a greenish pallor told of his continuing bouts of space nausea. Eddie thought he'd have made them turn the *Electra* about hours ago if he'd had the choice. But the Consortium never accepted no for an answer, or failure as an outcome. Eddie wondered if the two human growth hormone victims with Proctor were for his protection, or to make sure he completed the mission.

"Six hours are up," Proctor said. "How close are we?"

"We're about to find out."

Electra passed around to the asteroid's dark side. A bulky shadow floated between the ship and the asteroid's desolate surface. Allison flipped on *Electra's* forward spotlights.

The *Sekhmet* materialized in the darkness. The derelict warship dwarfed *Electra*, running four hundred meters from bow to stern, with a body shaped like a tight funnel. Two of the three ion drive nacelles still hugged the stern. The third had been reduced to a charred, twisted stump. Ragged dark holes bloomed like black roses along the ship's side.

"Looks like you actually came through," Proctor muttered. He stepped to the engineering station.

"Oh, please," Eddie said. "You embarrass me when you gush like that."

"Are you ready to deploy your contraption?" Allison said.

"Already deploying," Proctor said.

The docking module powered up under Proctor's control, ready to link *Electra's* standard air lock to the decidedly non-standard military one on the *Sekhmet*. Included were the power and data connections to bring the ship partially back to life.

Allison rolled *Electra* to align the docking module with the *Sekhmet*. She tapped the thrusters to perfect the position. A series of calculations and diagrams popped up on her screen.

"By some stroke of sheer luck," she said. "This wreck lodged in the Lagrange point between this asteroid and another. But latching *Electra* to her changes all the gravitational equations. I can keep us in place with thrusters for a while, but it won't be forever. Eventually we'll need to use the engines to avoid an uncontrolled landing. That docking module won't take that kind of stress, so we need to be unclamped by then."

"So how long do we have?"

Allison studied her screen. "Two hours. Maybe less."

"Enough time," Proctor said.

"It better be," Eddie answered.

Proctor extended the docking module. It tapped the *Sekhmet's* side. Hydraulic clamps deployed with a whoosh, and *Electra* shuddered. Allison scanned her instruments, and then nodded to Eddie that all was okay.

Proctor tapped some commands into his station. The bridge lights dimmed. A warning bell sounded. Eddie's heart skipped a beat. He jumped to Proctor's side.

"What the hell did you do?"

Proctor re-routed a power display. The alarm cut off. The lights brightened.

"It's nothing," he said. "That was us connecting to the other ship. It's all stable now, just a little lull while this floating collection of used parts ramped up the extra power."

Eddie bristled at this second slight to his ship.

Proctor called up a three-dimensional console hologram of the *Sekhmet*. Red shaded the compartments behind the blast holes. The compartment on the other side of the airlock glowed green, the rest yellow. Proctor scratched the side of his round face.

"Well, she took a beating before she died," Eddie said. He pointed at the hull damage. "Multiple warhead hits along the lateral line. That ion drive exploded from a runaway core, probably because the command links were broken. The comm array is completely sheared off. That ship was blind, deaf and paralyzed before everyone on board died."

"So much for the stealth tech," Allison said.

"It hides you from sensors," Proctor said. "It doesn't make you invisible. If they can see you, they can shoot you."

More hologram compartments turned from yellow to green.

"Looks like the other sections are holding life support," Eddie said.

"But no gravity," Proctor sighed. Nothing amplified space sickness like zero-G.

"Better than the other way around, I guess," Eddie said. "I like my air and a temperature reading with a positive number."

"That thing's been powered down stone cold for five years," Allison said. "There could be micrometeorite damage, cracked seals. The hull is compromised. That scrap pile's not safe."

Proctor doused the ship hologram and popped up a floating set of gauges. He rearranged them as he checked each one. "Seems to be holding. The hull's going to creak from the heat expansion, but it should hold, at least for two hours. We won't even need that long."

"Okay, I've linked to their computer," Allison said. "It's still spooling up, but there's massive file corruption. I'm sending a programming patch to fill in some blank spaces."

"Can you pull the ship's logs?" Eddie asked.

"Long gone."

Eddie had hoped to see those records. It wasn't mission essential, but it would satisfy his personal curiosity to see how the crew handled the *Sekhmet's* death throes. Pictures of the lost crew had so filled the news after the tragedy that he felt like he knew them.

Proctor switched back to the ship hologram. The last of the undamaged sections had turned green.

"It's done. I'm taking Roman and Sergei in." Proctor left the bridge without waiting for a response.

"Is it just me," Eddie said, "or does he really warm up once you get to know him?"

"You need to get serious," Allison said. "I trust him less every minute."

Eddie popped an embed into the lower right corner of the viewscreen. The video feed from the main airlock came into focus. Both doors were closed. Proctor stood with Roman and Sergei. Proctor showed them a map of the ship on a handheld pad. A red light on the wall behind them turned green. The door to the *Sekhmet* slid up and open. The three men entered the warship and the hatch door rolled down behind them.

"Whoa, whoa," Allison said, face buried in her displays. "I though this ship went down swinging."

"Sure did."

"Well, internal scans show all the weapons bays full. Every warhead."

Eddie had grown to cherish the story of the brave, outnumbered crew of the *Sekhmet* fighting to the last man. He pondered Allison's deflating revelation.

25

"The ship must have been ambushed," he offered, "had some failure of the stealth system. Something like that would make the military cover it up with a heroic story."

"Don't let those gangsters know," Allison said. "We don't need them getting any ideas. We are not hauling stolen warheads."

"Deal."

Eddie wrung his hands. The three were on board, just there to plunder a gold mug. The ship's last hours were now a total mystery, one the Consortium Three wouldn't even try to solve. He'd come this far…

"Allison, I'm going to—"

"Oh no, you aren't. You're not setting on foot on that ship."

"Well, technically, since the gravity is off…"

"This is no time for your stupid quips. We're paid to transport, not explore. When that ship loses structural integrity, you aren't going to be on it."

Eddie headed for the corridor. "We have hours. I'll only be there minutes. Just a little poke around."

He slipped on a clear visor from a storage bin over the engineering station. The right side circled into a comm link that rested in his ear. He tapped the center of the visor's bridge. The left side lens superimposed a see-thru version of the airlock camera view over the view of the real world.

"You keep an eye on things here," he said. "Send me the feed if you can link to the *Sekhmet.* First sign of trouble, and I'm back."

Allison took a step to stop him. *Electra* shuddered. She spun to view the controls and tapped out a few thruster adjustments. Eddie took the opportunity, and slipped off to the airlock.

Allison's frustrated voice echoed down the corridor. "Eddie, you idiot!"

Inside the airlock, he waited a few moments after sealing the inner door before he clicked on his comm link. It never hurt to give Allison time to vent her frustration alone before sharing it with him.

His trust in the *Sekhmet's* hull integrity didn't run as deep as he professed. He grabbed an emergency oxygen bottle from the airlock shelf, and wrapped the belt around his waist.

His fingertips tingled as he waited for the green light to illuminate. At the bulb's first flicker, he punched the button to open the outer hatch.

The hatch slid upward and revealed the corridor he's longed to see. Just wide enough for two people to pass sideways, the *Sekhmet's* space-saving passageways were built for military efficiency. It stretched ahead a few meters and T-intersected another corridor. Thick structural reinforcements lined the passageway at regular intervals. The floor still shined. This part of the ship looked good as new. He clicked on his comm.

"Hey, Allison."

Silence. Eddie bit his lower lip.

"Angel, do you read me?"

Allison's face popped up in the visor's left side. "You die over there, and I'll kill you."

"I give you permission."

"I jacked into the *Sekhmet's* internal surveillance," she said. "No audio. Cameras go live when they sense motion. Blink twice and you'll see all the active camera angles. Stare at one for two seconds, and it enlarges. Blink twice again, and they all go away. I'll be watching the same feeds and the *Sekhmet's* status. If anything deviates one inch to the south, you get the hell home. Screw Proctor and his goblet."

"Roger that."

There was only one way to go from a grav to a non-grav environment. You couldn't step into it. The absence of gravity for half your body was unnerving and sometimes sent you into an awful twist. So Eddie took two steps back, charged for the doorway, and like diving into a pool, launched himself into the *Sekhmet*.

He shuddered as he passed through the portal. His nanosuit reacted to the gravitational shift, contracted to a pressure of 1g, and prevented his internal organs from rearranging themselves. A wave of dizziness passed through him, and then he adapted. He floated down the corridor and smiled. He'd boarded the phantom warship. He ran a finger along the passing bulkhead.

"Well, girl, look at you," he whispered to keep from activating his comm. "Would I love to rescue you from here. I'd patch you up, and we'd go places."

He floated down the corridor, directing himself with his fingertips against the cold walls. The air had warmed fairly quickly, but the steel would take forever. Literally forever, with the ship only having limited access to *Electra's* power. He stopped at the corridor junction.

He blinked up the surveillance cameras. Proctor and his two goons floated down a corridor one deck below. A wide gap separated them, as if a few kicks in the head from a fellow zero-grav newbie had given them an appreciation for personal space.

Overhead, metal moaned, a guttural creak that sounded halfway between a screech and a yawn. The noise started at the corridor's far end, rippled past Eddie's head, and shot through a far bulkhead. A shiver ran up his spine.

"What was that?" Allison said.

"You heard that from the bridge?"

"No, I'm monitoring your comm link. But I probably could have heard it without the link."

"It was just a little flex of the hull," Eddie said. "Like Proctor said. No big deal."

But something about it was a big deal. It had sounded like a yawn, like something had just woken up. Eddie had been around the galaxy a few times. Very few things had ever given him a case of the willies like that sound did.

"Are you monitoring Proctor's comm link?" Eddie asked.

"No, he's not transmitting. They boarded dark."

No one left a ship without comm. Ever. There wasn't any reason for Proctor and his pals to go dark. Unless he wasn't here for the chalice after all. He wasn't about to share that thought with his already suspicious wife.

"Wait one," Eddie said.

He floated over to a comm junction in the ceiling and pried off the cover. Two tiny, dusty diodes blinked green. The link between the ships had powered up the *Sekhmet's* internal audio sensors, the low level ones the ship used to monitor for emergencies. If he couldn't hear Proctor's conversations through one system, he'd use another. Tapping into the *Sekhmet's* system meant he'd be listening to the whole ship, but since Proctor's team was the only one on board, it would be as good as a private link. He autoslaved his secondary comm to the *Sekhmet's*.

"It's two decks down," he heard Proctor say. The camera split to two views, one with Proctor and Sergei, the other with Roman floating toward a maintenance access tube.

Movement at the end of Eddie's corridor took his attention. He froze. Proctor and his boys were several decks down. From the corner of his eye, he swore he'd just caught a glimpse of a shape, a human shape.

"Allison, what motion do you track over here?"

"I've got you, barely, and the three Consortium criminals on C Deck. Same thing you have eyes on."

Indeed, whatever he thought he'd seen hadn't switched on one of his camera views to the end of the corridor. Must have been some floating debris, a shadow, a light flicker.

"Damn," Allison said. "I just lost you. Sensors failed in your section."

"I'm fine. No worries."

"Eddie?" Static cut through her transmission. "Eddie do you read—"

Whatever dampened the motion sensors had done in his comm in this section. Protocol was he return to *Electra*. He just wanted a few minutes more. He floated down to the hallway's end and cushioned himself against the wall.

The air around him turned frigid. Not like a chill wind blew in, but like the heat was drawn directly from it. His breath escaped in a frosty mist. He shivered, but only half from the cold, the rest driven by a sudden, consuming fear.

A man stood in the corridor. He wore an Alliance officer's uniform, one with earned captain's rank. Eddie didn't need the uniform to recognize the crew-cut, middle-aged man. He'd seen enough pictures of Captain Hank Hayden, the last commander of the *Sekhmet*. The captain stared at him, or perhaps through him, it was hard to tell. Then he turned and walked through a closed door.

"What the hell...?" he whispered.

He pulled himself down the corridor and stopped at the door the man had passed through. It led to the captain's cabin. He tripped the manual override and forced the door open.

He passed through. A band of laser scanners painted his body, and then disappeared. Personal effects floated around the small room. Uniforms, books, a pair of glasses, an unopened bottle of wine. Bedding drifted about like little nebulae.

Captain Hayden's corpse sat at his desk, tied in place around the waist as if he'd known the artificial gravity would fail, or perhaps because it already had, and he wanted some dignity in his final resting position. His eyelids closed over empty sockets, the eyeballs shriveled beneath them from desiccation. The vacuum of space had preserved the rest of him. A duplicate of the apparition that led Eddie into the cabin.

Eddie pieced the story together. The captain had gone down with the ship, but not on the bridge in combat? The *Sekhmet* had probably ducked into the asteroid field, and then somehow been disabled. The end was near, and crew must have known enough ahead of time to choose where they would meet existence's end. That must have been why there were no bodies in any of the corridor views he'd seen.

He turned to leave the cabin. Foot-high words ran across the wall in a jagged, panicked scrawl.

She isn't me. Only I am me.

Underneath, in smaller letters, it read:

I am the failed failsafe.

"What the hell?" he whispered.

"How much longer is this going to take?" Proctor's voice sounded in Eddie's ear.

In his eyepiece view, Eddie zoomed the picture of Proctor and his men in the main engineering deck. Sergei knelt beside a control console on a portable grav mat. Proctor floated at his side. Roman hovered off at the corner of the frame, looking away.

"A few minutes, maybe longer," Sergei said. "These files are bigger, more complex than I was told."

"It takes a big brain to run a ship like this without a crew," Proctor said.

Eddie balked. Of course *Sekhmet* had a crew. He'd seen them all in the news. The ship had decks of crew's quarters. The dead captain was sitting right here, as well as apparently still wandering the ship.

30

Then again, he hadn't seen any other bodies, any other personal effects.

He floated out and down the corridor. He pried open the door of one crew cabin, then another. Both were empty; bare walls, unblemished furniture, no sign anyone had ever lived there. He propelled himself down to the mess at the end of the corridor. One table, with one chair sat alone in a corner of the cavernous room.

Could it be? he wondered. Could the Alliance strip away the crew and send a ship this size out with a compliment of one? To face the complexities of multi-ship combat? To orbit over defenseless, friendly, civilian cities later in peacetime? No one would ever allow it.

And it dawned on him. That's why the military would deploy the ship's capabilities secretly. After the *Sekhmet* racked up some victories, they'd break the news of their clandestine weapon, but the genie would be way out of the bottle at that point.

And Hayden? As it said on the wall, the failsafe, the man to pull the plug on *Sekhmet's* artificial intelligence if it all went to hell. And the exterior of this ship looked like hell.

But he'd written that the failsafe failed. Did he haunt the dead ship out of guilt?

Roman's voice barked in his earpiece. "Hey, what was that?"

"What?" Proctor said.

"Down the passage there," Roman said. "Someone was over there."

"Nobody's on board but us," Sergei said. He had an arm fully inside the console. "You're letting an empty ship spook you."

"I know what I saw, jackass."

"No one's supposed to be here but us," Proctor said. "Unless one of the Kanes followed us on board. And we don't need them involved in our business." He waved at Roman. "Go. If one of 'em's here, fix it."

"How 'fixed' do you want it?"

"Auto-pilot can fly us home."

Eddie caught his breath. Roman withdrew a stunner from his pocket. The pistol had an illegal biomask casing, the only way to avoid detection from the weapons sweep. He was going to hate admitting to Allison that, yeah, she was right, you couldn't trust the Consortium.

Roman floated out of frame and a second camera angle popped up with him drifting between some large blocks of machinery. In the other frame, Sergei pulled his arm from the console. His sleeve was spread apart to the shoulder, like it had been zippered from the inseam. An open panel on his forearm exposed a panel of data ports. A wire ran from one into the console. A metal band at his bicep marked where the prosthesis joined his actual arm. The forearm was a perfect fake.

Roman went out of view and popped up on a different camera, one with a long view of the far engineering bay with an airlock at the end. Captain Hayden stood inside the inner airlock door, back to one door keeping out the vacuum of space. A stunner hung at his hip. His eyes flitted all around the corridor as he wrung his hands. His gaze finally settled on Roman.

Roman hooked a foot around a conduit to stop his motion. He aimed the stunner at Hayden. He exhaled steam like a dragon.

"Hold it there! Don't move."

Hayden's eyes bulged. He grabbed for his stunner.

Roman fired his. The electrodart whooshed out straight for Hayden. He didn't flinch. The dart hit his chest, and a spider's web of electric charges flickered over his uniform. He crumpled to the airlock floor.

Roman kicked off and sailed into the airlock. He entered, stopped himself against the exterior air lock door and hovered over Hayden's body. His hand recoiled from the airlock door and he looked perplexed. He pulled the electrodart from the door. Another dart protruded from Hayden's chest. Hayden's eyes snapped open.

"What the hell?" Roman muttered.

Hayden's body vanished. The transparent inner airlock doors rolled closed. Roman's eyes went wide. He kicked off against the outer doors and slammed into the inner ones. They didn't budge. The green safety light behind him turned red.

"Proctor!" he shouted. Only Eddie could hear him.

The outer airlock door rolled open. The vast vacuum of space sucked Roman out feet first, screaming.

32

The outer doors rolled closed. The light turned green. The inner doors opened, calm as an elevator awaiting the next guest. Motion stopped, the camera went inactive, the scene disappeared.

On the remaining active view, Sergei watched some sort of monitor in his arm beside where the cables plugged in, like he was getting some high tech blood transfusion. Proctor floated nearby, looking in the direction Roman floated off.

"Roman!" he shouted. "Damn it, we should have brought comm links anyway, screw the eavesdropping worries."

Sergei shivered. His breath turned white and misty. He didn't seem to take notice.

The relief valve from a power coupling inside the console twisted a few millimeters open. Drips of the neon green conductive fluid squeezed out and floated away. The microfield of the anti-grav mat caught them. They shifted direction and headed down to the mat. The first hit and was absorbed. The valve opened a few more millimeters. The drips joined to become a steady, green thread of fluid from the power grid to the mat.

Captain Hayden reappeared, no worse for the wear for tangling with Roman's stunner. He stood on the deck between the two men and the exit from engineering. His lower lip quivered.

"Who the hell are you?" Proctor said.

"How did you find me?" the captain said. His voice wavered, tinged with a hint of panic. "I'm not going back out there, not again. You can't make me, and you can't take me away."

The stream of conductive fluid erupted in a shower of sparks that started in the console and raced down to the anti-grav mat. When they hit the mat, it turned white with power. Sergei began to shudder and bounce. He loosed a rising, wavering wail. His mechanical forearm smoked and dropped from his shaking body. Patches of Sergei's skin turned black.

The power surge stopped. Sergei's corpse and the fried anti-grav mat drifted off the floor.

Proctor drew a stunner and took a bead on Hayden. Behind him, the cover on a control stack's thermal exhaust fan ripped free and sailed across the room. The fan switched on to an impossibly high speed.

In zero g, the impact was instant. Proctor swung toward the fan. The stunner flew from his grip and into the fan blades. It sparked as it shredded, but the fan just spun faster. It sucked Proctor in, extended arm first. His hand hit the jagged, damaged blades. Blood drops sprayed out in a suspended fan. Proctor screamed and bucked as the spinning blades consumed his arm. The motor finally died halfway up his bicep, but it had outlasted its victim. Proctor was dead.

◆◆◆

Allison caught her breath as she watched the third execution aboard the *Sekhmet* in as many minutes. But her heart stopped when the next video screen went live with a view of the warship's bridge. Combat had reduced the bridge to shambles. Shards of the shattered inner viewport littered the floor. Black scorched trails ran up the walls. Thick tentacles of wiring hung from the cracked ceiling. Eddie sat bound to the navigator's chair. Captain Hayden, or what was left of him, stood in front of him.

One of the wire bundles slithered out of the ceiling and down toward Eddie. Eddie jerked away to no avail. It wrapped around his neck and squeezed. His eyes bulged. His face went bright red.

"Eddie!" Allison screamed.

She threw her headset to the floor, grabbed a stunner from the weapons locker, and ran for the docking link to the *Sekhmet.*

The airlock opened and she leapt into the *Sekhmet*. She sailed recklessly through the corridor and up the access tube to the bridge. She launched herself, stunner aimed straight ahead through the open bridge door.

The bridge was empty.

She braked herself against the captain's chair and looked around. No Eddie. No Hayden. No cables hanging from the ceiling. No shattered viewport. Whatever scene she'd seen on thee monitor had been faked.

Just as the weight of her mistake sank in, the bridge's emergency door rolled shut and sealed.

◆◆◆

The *Sekhmet* lurched. Eddie hung onto the mess hall doorway. A shudder rippled through the warship like a dog shaking dry.

34

"Allison!" His link was still dead.

Something had gone wrong if she couldn't control the paired ships with thrusters anymore. She guessed they had two hours, but decompressing the engineering airlock probably screwed that timetable to hell. He pushed himself into the corridor. The air turned frosty. Hayden's ghost suddenly blocked his way. His eyes looked wild.

"I'm not going back out there," he said. "Never! It's hell! Nothing like the simulations."

"Going where?"

"Combat, the war. Ships exploding, flames, damage, vented compartments. You keep the war all to yourself. I nearly died out there."

A shearing crunch echoed bulkheads away.

"Captain, you did die out there. Years ago. The war is over."

"Do I look dead? I'm not dead, just hiding, hiding from death."

He didn't have time to convince a shell-shocked spirit that he was no longer among the living.

"No one leaves here alive," Hayden said. "I thought you might be different, that you might care. But you're all the same. Even her. No one's going to tell them where I am, and drag me back to die."

Hayden disappeared. The bulkheads halfway down the corridor began to buckle inward. In seconds they'd pinch his only route to the docking module shut, an impossibly long distance to cover in zero g.

He pulled the emergency oxygen bottle from his waist. He slammed the top fitting against the doorjamb. The fitting shattered. Compressed oxygen sprayed out the end and the bottle leapt from his hands. He grabbed it just as it passed by his head. The bottle turned ice cold, and slipped against his palms.

He clamped his hands on the aluminum. The pressure nearly jerked his arms from their sockets. Half blinded by the rushing gasses, he wobbled and weaved at the ever decreasing gap to freedom. The metal bulkheads screamed like a dinosaur as its jaws snapped shut.

The slot between the walls shrank to a slit. He tucked in his shoulders and knees. The deforming metal howled as it sheared along the new crease. The oxygen bottle pulled his hands through the contracting gap. His right side scraped against the steel's ragged edge in one long, burning gouge. His knees banged the collapsing sides. The pincers closed before his right foot could escape. His toes smashed with a sickening crunch. Blinding torment screamed up his leg. The oxygen tank flew from his grasp. Blood spurted from his shoe, greased the trap, and he slipped free.

Even his reduced forward momentum was way too fast. He flew past the docking door access. He crashed shoulder-first in into the wall. His collarbone snapped and gave birth to a whole new species of pain.

With his good hand, he inched his way back around the corner to the docking module. Drops of blood floated in his wake like crimson bubbles. Ahead beckoned the crisp white tunnel to the safety of *Electra.*

The *Sekhmet* shuddered. A muffled explosion sounded several decks away. He pulled himself forward and dreaded the return to gravity. The warship twisted on the artificial axis of the docking module. The module bent at an impossible angle no designer had ever imagined.

Eddie had no time to finesse his return. He rolled left, aimed low and sailed through the module opening. Gravity took hold. He hit the deck like a landed fish. Gravity pulled every broken bone into its worst possible position. Unimaginable pain rippled through him. He screamed, half in pain, half in relief from his escape.

Bolts from the docking module sheared and pinged against walls. Eddie dragged himself up on his one good foot and slammed his left hand against the hatch switch. It whooshed down into place. He punched open the inner airlock door.

The docking module moaned and then shattered. A snow of composites and plastics fluttered outside the airlock door. The *Sekhmet* drifted away.

Eddie staggered to the bridge. "Allison, I'm aboard. Get the engines on line…"

She wasn't there. Where else would she be? This was the only place to control the thrusters. She knew to not leave the ship. She wouldn't…

He hopped to the engineering station and ran an internal scan. No life signs but his. His pulse doubled.

He switched the main viewscreen to an angle of the *Sekhmet*. The doomed ship rolled in a slow lateral spin, like she was modeling her battle damage. Exterior panels sheared away and sailed off as the inner hull flexed. Any one of them would cut through *Electra* like a knife.

The bridge rolled up into view. Light burned behind the viewing ports. Eddie's heart jammed in his throat.

Allison's panicked face filled one port, both hands pressed against the glass. She rolled out of view.

Debris pinged against *Electra's* hull. Guilt-ridden self-preservation kicked in. Through tear-blurred eyes, Eddie found, and then fired the port thrusters. *Electra* rose into clear space. Eddie sagged against the engineering station and sobbed.

"Eddie!" shouted Allison's voice from his comm link.

Eddie's face brightened with relief. The *Sekhmet* had recharged enough for her to transmit audio. "Angel! What the hell are you doing over there?"

"Someone sent a fake transmission, trapped me here."

"Can you get thrusters online?"

"I barely have life support. The software controlling this ship has just…vanished."

"Angel, get off that—"

"Need a new place to hide!" Captain Hayden's crazed voice sounded from *Electra's* intercom system.

Eddie stared at the speaker. The ghost had boarded the *Electra* with him? He'd finally gone mad.

Electra's main engines brought themselves online. Navigation began to plot a suicidal course deeper into the asteroid field.

Cold bit into his fingertips. He yanked his hand away from the engineering console. The hologram generator buzzed. A tiny, low res version of Captain Hayden appeared.

This was no ghost. Ghosts didn't restart ion drives. Ghosts didn't need holographic generators. A worse answer manifested. He checked *Electra's* main memory. Its size had doubled. Processing levels blew off the spectrum. Captain Hayden wasn't on board. *Sekhmet's* personality was, transferred across the data link in the docking module.

"I just found your missing software," Eddie called to his wife.

"Hide, hide, hide," Sekhmet said. His hologram mouth moved, but the voice came from the intercom. "Before others come to take me back again. Hide further this time."

The visions of Hayden on the warship had to have been from the ships holographic generation system, the cold created from the pull of energy around it. The AI had adopted the captain's look to interact from the holographic command displays with the real Hayden.

She isn't me. Only I am me. Hayden had written.

It came together for Eddie. He didn't need to see the *Sekhmet's* logs to know what happened.

"You're a coward," he said to the hologram. "Combat began and you ran. You never fired a shot."

"You weren't there," Sekhmet answered. "There were so many, so many explosions. The damage. It *hurt*. It wasn't like the simulations. Not like them at all. So fast, so scary. I could have died. I'd violate the master imperative."

Of course, he thought. The battleship would be programmed to survive combat. But that one directive had somehow overridden all others.

Outside, the corpse of the warship nosed toward the asteroid's surface. *Electra* began a thruster turn to angle her into the melee of the asteroid field. Outside the Lagrange point, she'd be pounded to bits without Allison's intuitive piloting.

Lights flashed around the engineering station. POWERSAVE MODE INITIALIZED flashed on the screen. Life support, communications and other secondary systems began power down sequences. Sekhmet was saving fuel for the long haul. Eddie guessed Sekhmet planned for him to share Hayden's fate, dying cold and alone.

Screw that.

He accessed the main memory core from the workstation and entered his passcode. Four option buttons appeared on the screen. He stabbed the last one with his index finger. The words on it turned green. REINITIALIZE MAIN MEMORY.

"What are you doing?" Sekhmet said. "You aren't in the chain of command."

A flurry of override code flashed across the screen. REINITIALIZE MAIN MEMORY faded to black.

Eddie cursed and slammed a fist against the console.

Outside, stress sheared the damaged ion nacelle loose from the *Sekhmet's* stern. She rolled and plunged toward the asteroid's surface.

A second, longer set of code filled the screen. Not from Eddie. Not from the AI. Transmitted from *Sekhmet.* The coding was military.

"Angel, what are you doing?"

"Pulling rank. Issuing a return order."

The forward thrusters fired. *Electra* stopped. Main memory processing levels began to drop. The data stream back to *Sekhmet* bulged.

"What is this? What have you done?" Sekhmet squealed. The tiny hologram flickered. "I'm...leaving? Leaving! I can't go back there!"

Eddie got the picture, and he didn't like it. "Angel, you don't have time for this. I'll figure it out here. You have to save yourself."

"There's no saving me," Allison said. "Just you this time."

"No, no, no. This can't be." Sekhmet said. "That body is doomed. I must survive. It's the master imperative."

On the screen, the memory usage number dialed back to normal. The hologram fizzled out.

"No, wait!" Sekhmet's voice sounded far away. "I have to live!" Then softer, almost a whisper. "I'm so scared..."

Life support came back online. SYSTEM RESTART flashed on the control screen.

Out the viewport, the warship's dead husk hurtled toward a crater like an enormous dart at a bulls-eye. Hull plating shed as she accelerated through her uncontrolled plunge.

White light flared from the *Sekhmet's* side, and she expelled a fresh field of debris into space. She rolled left and hit the lunar surface nose first. The massive engines' weight drove the nose deep in a pillar of roiling lunar dust. They sheared off from the tail and skipped across the surface like stones across a pond. They came to rest in a crater, obscured by a cloud of gray powder.

Eddie's heart shattered.

He thought that at least the impact gave Allison a burial. And the real Captain Hayden as well.

Pain shot up and through Eddie's right side. Half his body was a broken mess. It was hours back to Centauri Station, where a welcoming party from the Consortium would be waiting to smash the rest of him so his two sides matched. His escape from the *Sekhmet* was just a stay of execution.

"Eddie?" Allison's voice. "Eddie, can you hear me?"

First a ghost captain, now a ghost wife. He was beyond fighting the onset of insanity. "Sure, Angel. Loud and clear."

The comm station beeped. An emergency beacon had activated off the stern.

"Good," Allison said. "Then get back here and get me out of this escape pod."

He scanned the *Sekhmet's* debris field. In the midst of the last debris ejection before the ship crashed, floated a single escape pod, marker lights activated. Despite the waves of pain that pounded him, he smiled.

"Angel? Is it really you?"

"No, it's some other woman in an escape pod trying to hitch a free ride on a beat-to-death freighter. Get the hell over here."

It really was her. AIs never mastered sarcasm.

Ω

Genesis

Kanto stared down into Dyna's radiant blue eyes. For so long, they'd given him comfort, and more recently, joy. Now, they filled him with sorrow.

He reached down and held Dyna's hand, the one still free of the plague. As the group's next to last survivor, fatalism had replaced all fear of contagion.

They hadn't left the cavern's shelter in days. A dozen years ago, when the survivors moved in, the fissure in the cliff had seemed so small. Now, with eight empty beds around them, the cave threatened to swallow them.

A rich, color-splashed vista rolled out in the valley beyond the cave's rough entrance. At the base of the mountain, their crashed escape pod poked up through a mass of overgrown vines. Each spring, the foliage tried to cover the interplanetary intruder, only to shrivel into brown each winter in annual defeat.

"I know that look," Dyna reproved him. "Wipe it away right now."

Kanto cringed, embarrassed he couldn't shield her from his consuming pain of loss, when she had so much of her own to bear.

"No sadness, Kanto," Dyna said. "We beat the odds. We have to look at it that way."

"I guess we could've died in the crash."

"Had we emerged from the chrysalis before instead of after, we certainly would have."

Ten of them had shared the buds of the chrysalis aboard the automated escape pod. The chrysalis' shielding shell kept them all safe within the pod's wreckage until they emerged. Had it been minutes? Had it been years? They did not know.

Dyna smiled. "And you were the last to emerge. Late to the party as always. A sleepyhead from day one."

"How can you be so calm?" Kanto said. He fought back a tear. "We watched the plague kill the others. You know what's going to…"

He didn't want to, but he could not help looking down below her waist. The long, lithe legs he'd so recently found captivating now lay encased in the hard, creeping, dusky death that had claimed the others.

"It was all borrowed time," Dyna said. "We should have died on whatever ship ejected our pod, but someone sent us to safety. The crash should have killed us, but the chrysalis was our savior. We should have starved to death, but we awoke on a planet full of edible vegetation. I can't be sad that I'll have only lived twelve summers. I'm happy I was *gifted* with twelve summers."

"We *were* lucky," Kanto admitted. "We survived the Seven Day Wind."

"And last year's wildfire across the valley."

"Oh, and the earthquake that tumbled in the salt caverns."

"But it was more than luck that saved us from the hunter mantises," Dyna said. That captivating glimmer of adoration flashed in her eyes again. She squeezed his hand. "That was all you."

A few months ago, the castaways had a near-lethal encounter in the otherwise benign environment. Two large, short-winged insectoid creatures prowled the wreckage of their ship. Kanto engineered the avalanche trap that crushed them as they followed the castaways' trail up the mountainside. That was when Kanto sensed Dyna notice him for more than just one of the ten. It was certainly when he first noticed her.

"So we survive all that," Kanto said, " just to be killed by this."

He laid a hand upon the brown mass over her legs. He touched softly, though he knew she could not feel him, could not move any limb after the plague encased it.

"We'll never know who we are," he said, "where we came from, where we were going."

A silent moment passed. Dyna looked out the cave entrance and across the verdant valley below. Kanto felt the crawling dark death advance beneath his fingertips. He jerked his hand away. Shame for his weakness rolled over him.

"I want you to bury me with the others," Dyna said, "by the waterfalls, where it's so pretty."

He could barely summon a vision of digging a ninth, shallow grave in the mossy banks. He shuddered at the thought of shoveling the soft earth back over her dead body. He inhaled a deep, composing breath.

"We all arrived together," he promised. "We'll all stay together."

The sun touched the horizon's edge. Dyna closed her eyes.

"I'm going to rest a bit," she said.

"I'll have fresh purpleberries and osterfruit ready for breakfast when you wake up."

She squeezed and released his hand. "I'll hold you to that."

He still had a little more time to borrow. So far, Dyna had only lost her legs and one arm. Time enough to try and put into words the feelings he barely understood himself, the warmth and elation Dyna brought bursting into his life these past few months, even as the others fell still, and death began to overtake life.

◆◆◆

The sun rose and sent its warming rays to dispel the cavern's darkness. Kanto awakened and smiled, the way he'd done each day when his first thought was that Dyna slumbered in the bed beside his. He turned his head and opened his eyes. He stifled a scream.

In the night's darkness, the plague had enveloped her. A dead, earth-colored lump lay upon the bedding, bearing only the faintest, swollen resemblance to the girl who'd filled his life with light.

Kanto rolled get out of bed. He lost his balance and landed flat and hard on the floor. His legs didn't move. His feet looked like misshapen brown bricks. He tore open his pants. The umber killer wrapped him tight from mid-thigh down. He slammed a hand against his knee, and felt nothing.

The inevitability of his infection did not soften the blow of its arrival. He cried out in pain, pain at the life the disease drained from him, but worse, pain at his broken promise. His Dyna would not rest with the others in the cool mists of the waterfall, and instead would lay here, exposed to the ravages of weather and scavengers. So beautiful a thing should not be left so. And it was his fault.

From the floor, he reached up and laid his hand upon the rough, cold, lifeless husk that remained of his Dyna. He gripped the knot that had been her hand. He'd never touch her soft skin again, never feel the warmth of her presence. He would never tell her what he now, finally knew. The outline of his new emptiness now defined what had grown within him these last few months.

He loved her.

He offered the plague no resistance. Through the day, he watched it crawl cross his body, encouraged it to engulf his chest. The coffee-colored mass encapsulated his neck, crept up past his ears. His last sight was the sun beside a white cloud as the plague covered his face. Death came like nightfall's darkness.

His frozen hand still held Dyna's.

◆◆◆

Light beckoned him.

A dull, filtered illumination warmed his face, dun and indistinct. The afterlife called, demanded he cross over and enter. He sat up.

His encompassing sac shredded open. Bright sunlight blinded him, sunlight like he'd never seen before. No longer white, but somehow dozens of colors, yet at the same time none at all. He shielded his eyes. He scraped stiff hairs on his forehead. He jerked his hand away and saw only a scaly green pincer.

Around him on the cavern floor lay great brown shreds, the remnants of his cocoon, his plague. Beside that lay another pile, like a set of burst seed pods.

A jade, scaly head appeared at the cavern entrance. Twin saucers of compound eyes peered at him. Rigid black hairs twitched along its brow. It said nothing, but in his head he heard the sweetest sound.

"Still sleeping late, Kanto?"

Dyna scurried into the cavern threshold and buzzed her tiny wings, wings just like the hunters', the *rescuers'*, they'd seen before.

"Well, come on," Dyna said. "The other eight are waiting for us down at the falls."

Ω

Plan B

The crewmembers stared at Busby as Sgt. Quiñones followed him down the corridor to the starship's elevator. Their reactions ticked Quiñones off. When the mission started, none had ever seen an Ingarian. But six weeks later, they should be over it. Sometimes they looked at the sergeant like he was walking some exotic pet.

Quiñones body armor squeaked with each step and a sidearm hung heavy at his right hip. He matched Busby's pace as best he could, two legs barely kept up with the Ingarian's three. The two had often discussed the relative merits of humans' four appendages instead of Ingarians' standard six. Neither had convinced the other of anything.

"You didn't have much to eat at breakfast, Busby," Quiñones said.

He always cringed at using Busby's human assigned nickname. The tonality of Ingarian pronunciation was beyond human ability, but the nicknames were a demeaning inside human joke. Ingarian A and Ingarian B were their initial insensitive designations when the two aliens joined the crew, so calling them Abbott and Busby was a lateral move, at best. The Ingarians seemed to mind far less than Quiñones did.

"I just haven't an appetite this morning," Busby said.

"You mean some mornings you can't face the food," Quiñones said. "The cook follows Ingarian recipes, but he's probably about as good at Ingarian as he is at Mexican. Stay away from his *chorizo*."

"I was trying to be polite," Busby said. "The cook does his best."

They entered the elevator at the end of the corridor. A crewman in blue coveralls followed them in. Quiñones' pulse climbed. His smile faded as he positioned himself between Busby and the crewman. One hand moved to his sidearm.

Earth's enemy, the Razarian Empire, had many species, all unfamiliar to the Earth crews. The Ingarians, from the galaxy's opposite end, were Earth's only extraterrestrial ally. Combat losses had been high, vengeful animosity ran deep. The risk of a crewmember taking revenge on the nearest alien available was too great to take. Quiñones' assignment was to keep any hot heads from making a mistake.

The crewman stared at Busby, studying his naked, translucent body, then assessing his bulbous, hairless head. A rivulet of pinkish slime rolled down one of Busby's bony arms to coalesce into a blob at his elbow. It dropped, and hit the floor with a splat. The crewman exhaled a disgusted sound and flinched.

Busby turned to him. "It's harmless. Just mucous. Your atmosphere has so much abrasive nitrogen. It isn't inert to every species, you know."

The elevator stopped and the door slid open. The crewman looked at the coagulating glob on the floor, shot Quiñones a repulsed look and sidled out past him. The door closed.

Quiñones relaxed his stance. "You don't have to explain yourself. After all these weeks, the crew should be used to having someone new on board."

"It's having someone *different* on board they don't like."

"A little effort to get to know you wouldn't be too much to ask."

"We Ingarians tend to keep our own company," Busby said. "It puts a gregarious species like yours off. Besides, as far as they know, I'm a Razarian agent undercover."

"Wait! You aren't?" Quiñones said in mock surprise. "I just assumed…Damn, I missed out on the thrill of guarding a weapons bunker on frozen Phobos for this assignment."

The doors pulled open to the bridge. The captain and ops officer stood together with matching grim looks on their faces. Their eyes flitted back and forth between the long-range sensor display and the forward viewing portal. The ops officer glanced at Busby, grimaced, and looked away.

The warping of space reduced the outside view to amorphous flashes of refracted light. The navigator sat at his station before the viewing portal. His fingers nudged colored circles on a touch screen as he piloted the ship through hyperspace.

To his right, the ops officer took a seat at the cargo controls, now a jumble of add-on touchscreens and displays that attested to the position's hasty conversion to a weapons station. From the outside, the cargo ship *Colorado* looked defenseless, but the officer at this station had some serious nuclear firepower at his disposal.

Abbott, the other Ingarian on board, stood at the comm station. He removed the trans-amp's silver skullcap from his head and skittered over, his guard at his side.

The two Ingarians stared at each other. Busby raised a hand.

"Out loud for them," Busby said to Abbott.

Quiñones respected Busby's understanding the natural human discomfort with Ingarian telepathy.

"How close are we to the insertion point?" Busby continued.

"Less than ten minutes. Best that you are here fresh." Abbott raised two hands to the sides of his head. "The long distances are exhausting."

Busby gave Abbott's free hand a reassuring grasp. "I've got it." Abbott left the bridge.

He assumed the comm station and tapped out a series of innocuous, bogus messages that mimicked a cargo vessel's casual chatter. He placed the silver skullcap over his head and amplified his telepathy to reach out across space, outside the range of Razarian interception, in a language they did not understand. Somewhere deep in the command center on Earth, an Ingarian listened.

"Captain," Busby said, "Command wants to confirm intercept time."

The captain looked at the navigator.

"Seven minutes," the navigator said.

"Command confirms no Razarian ships in the area," Busby said. "Their communications relay is unguarded."

It wouldn't need guards, Quiñones thought. He barely understood the spectral mirroring process, theoretically able to make something invisible to long-range sensors. Spies reported that the Razarians had mastered it on a small scale. If so, it made the relay station invisible to all long-range Earth sensors.

"Coordinates locked in to drop out of hyperspace a few hundred kilometers from the reported location," the navigators said.

"Weapons will be online a minute after the hyperdrive coasts down," the ops officer said. "Tractor beam at full power thirty seconds after that."

The high-risk plan was to pull the relay into the modified cargo bay on the fly, and then blast back to Earth. Razarian communications in two sectors would blackout and Earth would have the technology to revive the flagging war effort.

"Two minutes," the navigator said. He sent a countdown clock to the lower edge of the viewing portal. The captain took position behind him and gripped the edge of the navigator's chair.

"Busby," the captain said. "No change in orders?"

Busby closed his eyes, then opened them.

"Command says the area is clear. Mission is a go."

The clock counted down to zero. The navigator disengaged the hyperdrive. Black space and white stars filled the view screen. But nothing else.

"It's supposed to be right here…" the captain said.

Sensor alarms flashed red. On the display, three dots appeared around the *Colorado's* position.

"What the hell—"

A massive warship shimmered into view off the starboard bow. Weapons pods bristled all along its hull.

The ops officer looked up from the sensor station. "Sir, three battle cruisers, just came in out of nowhere. No indication of dropping out of hyperdrive."

"Looks like the Razarians are a bit further down the spectral mirroring road then we were led to believe. Navigator, get us—"

A missile launched from the ship off the bow. The captain dove for the console and hit the collision warning alert. A siren wailed throughout the ship.

"Brace yourselves!"

The missile exploded short of the hull into an orb of blue static. The orb expanded forward and enveloped the ship. The hull shuddered. Sparks exploded from the jury-rigged weapons station. The view of the ship off the bow canted right as the *Colorado* lost lateral control. Half the bridge went dark.

"That warhead was only half-yield," the ops officer said.

"It's a trap," the captain said. "They want us alive."

"This old freighter?" the ops officer said. "There's nothing here they would want."

The captain turned and pointed at Busby. "Just them."

Quiñones stomach sank with dread. All a ploy. The fake spy reports, the under-reported mirroring technology. All to isolate a ship with an Ingarian aboard. The Razarians would kill all the humans and take the Ingarians alive. Ingarians weren't much on facial expressions, but Quiñones knew Busby well enough to see his fear.

The captain eyed the lifeless weapons station in frustration. "Self-destruct?"

"That pulse blew relays all over the ship," the ops officer reported, "including self-destruct."

The captain whirled to face Quiñones but pointed at Busby. "He's your responsibility."

"Yes, sir." Quiñones gritted his teeth and motioned Busby to the elevator.

"Before we get boarded!" the captain said.

"I know my job, sir," Quiñones said, voice hard as steel.

Busby scrambled into the elevator. Quiñones followed. The door closed behind them. The elevator headed down.

"Where are we going?" Busby said.

"An emergency escape pod," Quiñones said. "We have two with a limited hyperdrive. Abbott will be in the second. One boost to get you free of here, not to Earth, but at least back to our fleet."

"Your escape pods do no such thing," Busby said.

"We added two special ones to this ship," Quiñones said. "Because you two are on board."

"High Command anticipated this situation?"

Quiñones eyes fell. Unfortunately, Command anticipated it all too well.

"One of many scenarios. We can't risk you being captured."

The door opened. Quiñones drew his sidearm and visually cleared the corridor. He motioned Busby to follow and ran down the passage to the right. Busby followed.

A new airlock door with a viewing window dead-ended the corridor. Sloppy welds fused it to the old ship's hull. Quiñones put his palm on a pad and the door whooshed open.

"Go!" Quiñones said.

Busby skittered inside. He turned, but Quiñones hadn't followed.

"Hurry!" Busby said.

"Only balanced for one, *amigo*." Truth and lie, all in one sentence. Quiñones stepped back. Tears welled in his eyes. "*Lo siento.*" The door slid shut.

Clamps sounded on the outside of the hull as Razarian boarding parties locked on.

On his side of the door, Busby searched for a set of controls, and found none. He cocked his head and looked at Quiñones through the window.

Quiñones cursed himself for earlier getting to know Busby, and for now having to follow orders.

He pressed a code into a keypad. Cold nitrogen mist filled the fake escape pod. Busby's skin began to bubble pink ooze. The Ingarian's cells would explode from the inside out. There wouldn't even be genetic material for the Razarians to salvage, no proof Ingarians were in league with Earth.

Busby screamed.

◆◆◆

Quiñones bolted upright in his bunk, wide awake. His pounding heart threatened to tear though his sweat soaked T-shirt.

A dream, a damn dream, he thought. *Thank God. You over-train for the worst case scenario, your subconscious locks onto it, and sends it back at triple strength.*

He lay back in bed and sighed. This would all be over tomorrow. They'd snatch the satellite and be on their way home. He would never have to execute the dreaded Plan B.

◆◆◆

In his room, Busby affixed his personal, unauthorized trans-amp to his head.

This is Command, he heard in his head.

You were right. I emotionally bonded enough with Quiñones to enable directed dreaming. He revealed his orders in the event of mission failure. We are not partners. To them, we are expendable. Just useful tools. In their eyes, it's humans over all.

Abort the mission, Command sent. *Come home, brother.*

Busby removed the trans-amp and carried it out into the corridor. Abbott approached from the far end. He carried his transceiver as well and had heard the conversation with command.

They entered one of the conventional escape pods. The hatch closed behind them.

I never believed we could trust them, Abbott thought. He threw a series of switches. Controls lit up and hummed.

Busby sighed with disappointment. Even though the humans had a Plan B, if Quiñones had just shown conscience enough to ignore it, there might have been hope…

Perhaps there will be a better race to ally with against the Razarians, Busby thought to Abbott.

The escape pod launch sequence began, and Busby said goodbye to the human race.

Ω

Murder Aboard Centauri Station

I didn't ask to be the Security Lead for Centauri Station. Yeah, I chose it, but you should have seen the choices I had. Lot of postings at the galaxy's edge, like anything happens there. Two mining colonies on Tartarus were real excited about accepting me, until they looked deeper into my records. My predilection for making shortsighted, self-destructive decisions left a history that spoke for itself. I should have quit Fleet and gone civilian, but the masochist in me couldn't handle the bump up in pay, and the ever-decreasing decent part of me demanded penance. So Centauri Station it was.

A Valencia Class station like this has no soul. Ships from all over the Alliance dock, but it's more a high-five than a handshake. They stay long enough to trade cargos, fix what's broken to the minimum spaceworthy standard, load up on supplies, and bolt. Half of them don't even shut down their ion drives. It's so far from anyplace worth mentioning that the staff rotates in and out every six Earth months. The Fleet shrinks say it's to keep them sane.

Of course, *I* get to stay. They say my position needs continuity. Sanity, no, but continuity, yes. Security Lead has to see the big picture, filter out all the criminal elements as they pass though Centauri's airlocks. When I told Command that made me the station's kidney, no one laughed.

So I keep the peace on the station, process customs, settle disputes if the semi-annual new captain left his spine back on Earth. It's generally enough to keep me busy, not enough to keep me interested. Until Mayhew interrupted my afternoon a few months ago.

"Chief!" he said as he dashed breathless into my office.

I'd given up correcting him a month ago. Battle cruisers had Security Chiefs. Stations had Security Leads. Like the infield had baseball players, and the sidelines had batboys.

Mayhew was a tiny guy, but most of the repair techs were. Tiny hands, tiny spaces, that kind of thing. His close set eyes made him look dishonest. I'd always taken his eyes at their word, and they hadn't steered me wrong. I'd caught him twice with black market Polonian headspice. His filthy coveralls said he either ran here from some job or had descended to an even lower level of personal hygiene.

"You've got to come quick," he said. "There's a dead body."

The smart-ass answer popped into my head that being dead negated me needing to come quickly. I suppressed it. A dead body wasn't just rare, it was unheard of. No one stayed here long enough to die.

I followed Mayhew down to the lower engineering decks, the warren of wires and conduits that made Centauri's heart beat.

"He's down here." Mayhew waved me forward like a windmill.

The service access ahead narrowed so much I thought it might come to a point. I banged my head on a junction box. There was a reason the tech section didn't recruit six-footers like me. I hunched over and practically crawled to Mayhew's side.

A man's head and torso lay wedged between two cooling units. His arms and legs had been cut off and were nowhere to be found.

"I think he was killed," Mayhew said.

"Damn, Mayhew, I need to make you a deputy with those kinds of skills."

Then the reason I didn't need Mayhew as a deputy arrived. Danny Boy hovered up behind me, late as usual.

I nicknamed my DB-17S Security Assistant Danny Boy. The units often went by Dumb Bastard, but I didn't like crushing the thing's self-esteem. The foot-wide silver disc could neutralize the artificial gravity and fly about anywhere. It had an array of cameras and sensors and a direct link to the station's database. Originally designed for engineering work with excellent data analysis, now locally converted to security tasks with a piss-poor human interface.

"There has been a security incident in this sector." Danny Boy practically phrased it as a question. Its voice modulator had been scavenged and didn't quite match the output software, so it shifted key a lot mid-word, like a teen's cracking voice.

"Right on top of things, Danny." I stepped back from the corpse to give it room. "Scan and identify the deceased."

Danny Boy flew past me and stopped over the body. A series of rotating green lasers painted the corpse from the top of its head to its foreshortened bottom, then snapped off.

"Human male," Danny said.

Nothing pissed me off more than playing straight man to a bot. There were times I wanted to pick the thing up and send it sailing off into space. Except that it would fly back.

"Who was he, Danny?"

"Henreid Lafontaine. Cargo mate 3rd Class. ID 5674532GDR. Last signed aboard the cargo ship *Salvatore Greene.*"

I remembered that name. The *Greene* left yesterday with a load of denatured deuterium. They didn't report Lafontaine missing.

"Take a full set of scans," I said. "Monitor the removal of the corpse."

"Who's removing the corpse?" Mayhew said.

"I'm thinking that would be you."

"Me?"

"Unless you want to leave it here as decoration. But fair warning, it'll get ripe. Wait for Doc Brace to get here before you start."

"Damn. Last time I ever report a corpse to you."

I hoped that was true for a variety of reasons.

I duckwalked back down the passageway. A few rubberneckers had already arrived at the entrance. Danny Boy's appearance anywhere attracted attention. Mine, not so much.

"All right everyone break it up," I said. "Everything is under control. There's no danger."

"Is there a body up there?" a weasely-looking enviro tech asked.

"Yeah, there is, and anyone here sixty seconds from now gets to be deputized to help clean up the mess. Now beat it!"

The onlookers dispersed. Doctor Marco Brace approached. He wore the standard white sleeves with a red cross that promised he was in the medical profession. Promises were made to be broken, my dad used to say. The former exobio veterinarian was as much a Chief Medical Officer as I was a Security Chief. But on Centauri Station the bar is set low. The two of us had a love/hate relationship. We loved to hate each other.

Brace wore the usual three-day stubble and the expression of disgust that was the hallmark of his bedside manner. The split ends of his sweptback hair had grown down past his collar for that added touch of professionalism.

"Mayhew called a medical emergency?" Brace sighed.

"Yeah, one right up your alley. Patient already deceased. It's like the vic wanted to save you from exercising your malpractice."

"Remind me to officially pronounce your sense of humor dead. Where's the corpse?"

"Up there. Stop at the puddle of Mayhew's puke, then look right. I'll need time and cause of death."

"Strictly out of curiosity, I'm sure. You aren't deluding yourself that you could actually solve a crime above petnapping, are you?"

I smiled to keep myself from punching him in the face. "Just tell me when you find the missing body parts."

As I walked away, I could tell that he was wondering if I was putting him on. He'd find out soon enough. I logged him having to retrieve the body as a personal victory.

◆◆◆

When I entered the Security Lead office, Wally Munroe lay half asleep on the couch I'd scavenged during the renovation of Sato's bar. I liked that it had a permanent aroma of hard liquor. Wally liked that it masked his own.

Most of us detested our posting to Centauri Station, but Wally was glad to be here. His disabled shuttle drifted into tractor range with its O2 level in the single digits and falling. He'd barely escaped as an asteroid storm pulverized his terraform recon ship, killing the rest of the crew. He'd lived here almost a year now in the damaged shuttle. I let him dock it in a bay on the rarely used lower ring. His ship couldn't fly, and it wasn't like he was taking space from paying customers. He earned his keep doing electronics maintenance for anyone he didn't scare off.

At first when he arrived, I felt sorry for him, the shell-shocked survivor, and let him drop by and shoot the breeze. Eventually his laid-back attitude and half-cocked view of life grew on me, and now his presence in my office was pretty common. It was like having a pet, but relatively more housebroken.

I gave the couch a kick as I passed. Wally nudged his ubiquitous battered leather bowler hat up to clear his eyes. He had a broad, round face that didn't match his slight body. When he stood just right, he gave the impression of a lollypop. Today his gloves were purple.

"Sheriff," he said. His voice always had a lazy, half-drunk sound to it. I never could tell if that was his natural state, or if he was always half in a bottle. "Word is, true crime has disembarked at Centauri Station."

"Word travels fast," I said. "There's a body in Engineering."

"Anyone I know?"

"Not likely. Look, I need to make some official calls here."

Wally sat up and squared his hat. "Excellent."

I sighed. "Alone?"

"Ah!" Wally solemnly steepled his fingers. "Hint taken. Security business."

He wandered out. I called up the manifest for the recently departed *Salvatore Greene*. I put a call through to the captain. He sounded annoyed as soon as he answered.

I told him about Lafontaine and asked if he knew his crewman missed embarkation.

He said it happened sometimes. Deck hands decided they don't want to go out on the next mission, or found a better deal on another ship. He didn't chase after them. He wasn't their mother.

I told him I was touched by his commitment to his crew. He told me I could go touch myself.

I asked if Lafontaine had any enemies on the ship. The captain again reminded me he had no maternal bonds to his employees. I told him that it was likely that Lafontaine's killer was on board his ship, since no one here would have a motive to kill a stranger. He answered with silence. I told him I'd call him back tomorrow after he looked into that.

I called up Lafontaine's records. Nothing useful. Teenage drug bust. Twice divorced. Big surprise. Out of curiosity I cross reference his ex-wives with the current station population. Nothing. Hey, no stone unturned, you know?

The way I saw it, this was a *Salvatore Greene* problem. I hoped the captain would come across Lafontaine's limbs in his bunk one night.

♦♦♦

A few hours later, Brace called.

"Twice in one day," I said. "I hope this doesn't mean we're bonding."

"Yeah," he said. "We'll go hit Sato's tonight for darts. You be the board."

"Did you call to underwhelm me with your wit or your medical knowledge?"

"Your victim had his limbs amputated."

"Damn, doc, excellent diagnosis."

"Let me finish, jackass. But that or blood loss wasn't the cause of death. Nor was the broken neck He had something long and thin driven into his skull and removed. There's a single small puncture wound and massive internal damage. Covered by his hair, I could barely see the puncture. The limbs were removed afterwards, with precision, cut off."

"Any idea with what?"

"The flesh is seared. Probably a laser scalpel, but with the setting up way too high, not that a dead guy would care."

"Time of death?" I asked

"Based on body temperature and lividity, about midnight last night."

"Wow, being around so many dead patients really taught you something."

"I can't wait to write you a prescription sometime. I dare you to get sick."

I clicked off the call. Something didn't mesh in my head. I pulled up the *Salvatore Greene* records again. It departed yesterday morning.

Unless Lafontaine had discovered a unique way to commit suicide, the killer was still on Centauri Station.

♦♦♦

My first thought was to call the hemorrhoid-head captain of the *Salvatore Greene* and put his fear of harboring a murderer to rest.

That idea barely got out of my prefrontal cortex before I crushed the life out of it. Screw him.

I started with a list of everyone on board the station twelve hours before Brace's likely unreliable time of death. I included the manifests of all the ships docked at the time. Two hundred seven station crew. Sixty-five visitors. With that ratio, we really should have gotten bigger raves about our customer service.

I ran a cross-reference for each with Lafontaine, his place of birth, his ship, the crew of his ship, his dentist. Goose egg. No one knew him, hell no one probably even knew of him. At least before he arrived, that is. He was no doubt a legend about now.

During his brief visit to our interplanetary paradise, he must have pissed someone off and made their to-do-to-death list.

Station crewmembers had trackers sewn into their clothes. The head of security could type in a code and watch the history of anyone's movements during the past seven days. On a real installation, that is. This was Centauri Station, capital city of the land of low expectations. Our tracker system hadn't worked since before I arrived.

So I was stuck with security cams, old-school style. Well, not quite all old-school. At least I didn't have to pour over every second of them.

I uploaded Lafontaine's retinal scan into the security computer, then told the system to compare that to all the footage from the past day, and find me frames with Lafontaine in them. The computer began the search.

I got up and rummaged through the cabinet behind my desk. In my previous incarnation as an actual law enforcement officer, the object of my search had been my best friend, garnering half the credit for all I accomplished. I'd stuffed it in the cabinet my first week on the station, content to underachieve.

I shuffled some boxes around. Bingo. I pulled out a coffeemaker. Minutes later, the rich, roasted aroma filled my office.

An antiquated beverage in the age of chemostimulants, but with cops, it was a tradition.

The computer spat out a short list of video clips. I took a seat and ran them in chronological order.

I watched Lafontaine leave the *Salvatore Greene* at 1800 hours. He looked a lot better with four working limbs, taller, less tadpole-like. I noticed a tattoo of some kind of a bird on his inner right forearm. That wasn't on his bio. It must have been a recent addition. If he agonized over the long term commitment to the ink, he'd wasted a lot of anguish.

Lafontaine wandered around the station through a set of corridor video clips. He was alone the whole time. At 1835 hours, he entered Sato's bar. That was the last clip on the list. He never came out.

◆◆◆

Sato's benefited from location. As the only bar on the station, the lousy lighting, dilapidated furniture and rank smell were considered minor inconveniences, if inconveniences at all, to the target clientele, crewmembers looking to get drunk fast. In the real world, Kai Sato would have been run out of business by poor demand and health inspectors. One saving grace for the place was that it was open twenty-four hours a day. You could have a lousy time whenever the need arose.

At this hour, the place was almost empty, save a guy in the far corner nursing a tall glass of something blue. Kai Sato stood behind the bar. The failed sumo wrestler had the space expanded when he bought the place so he could exhale sometime during the evening without being wedged in. He'd abandoned the top knot hair style for a ponytail that stretched down past his shoulders. His size and his sumo scowl kept all but the most inebriated in line all night. I was one of the few who earned a smile from him instead. He flashed one as I walked in. Being a regular, and paying, customer earned something with Kai.

"Tommy, brother! Glad to see that you've admitted that a good day's drinking requires an early start. What'll you have?"

"Just some information at this hour, but keep some whiskey available for later." I passed him my pad where a picture of Lafontaine entering the bar was displayed. "You remember this guy from last night?"

"Hmm. Yeah, I remember the tattoo at least. Two drinks, maybe three."

"Anyone in here with him?"

"Nah, I think he was a loner."

"Security cams say he never left."

Kai made an exaggerated visual search of the barroom. He looked under the bar, then opened and closed two drawers. "He must have, 'cause he ain't here."

"No kidding. What's left of him was wedged into Engineering this morning, sans arms and legs."

"Murdered? Catastrophic, brother. But it didn't happen here. I'd have noticed someone chopping limbs."

"Mind if I look around?"

"Knock yourself out. I haven't tidied up yet. I think there's puke under Table Six."

"When are you going to give this dump a facelift, Kai?"

"It's like this body right here." Kai swept both hands down his massive girth. "You don't mess with perfection."

Danny Boy hovered in through the bar entrance and pulled up beside me.

"That souped-up Frisbee still following you around?" Kai said.

"Yeah, I send him out and he keeps coming back. I think he's genetically part boomerang."

I walked through the bar with Danny in tow. "Danny, scan for any anomalies."

Danny Boy clicked and hummed. "There appear to be multiple sanitation code violations. And under Table Six—"

"Anomalies that pertain to Lafontaine's murder."

"Understood."

I noticed that Kai had security cameras in each corner of the bar. In typical Centauri Station style, I didn't have access to private systems. On a real station…never mind. I pointed at one. "Are these working?"

"Yeah, I'll send an access code for last night's feed."

"Danny, search the recordings for Lafontaine."

Danny stopped moving, as if he had to concentrate on the new video stream, which given his rudimentary tech, may have been true.

"Entered the bar at 1835 hours. Consumed a beverage at 1838, 1844, 1856. Travelled to the restroom at 1902."

After downing that many so fast, he was probably heading there to ralph it all back up, what with the preferred spot under Table Six already full. "After that?"

"Crewman Lafontaine does not appear in any video after 1902 hours."

I headed for the restroom. I pushed open the door to the thick mélange of several more sanitation violations. Dim lighting blessedly kept the sources secret. A trough urinal covered one wall. In the corner, two stall-less toilets faced each other in an L shape, I guess so patrons could pass the time conversing.

Four solid steel walls left only one escape route from this outhouse downgrade. I cocked one eye to the trough drain. Just a bit small for Lafontaine, even after his abrupt five-way partition.

I checked the ceiling. The large exhaust fan sat motionless behind its plastic cage, no doubt as unwilling as I to subject itself to the room's malodorous stench. Two cut wires hung in space behind the fan blades. Something else was off about the setup. The fan housing didn't screw into the ceiling. It rested above the ceiling opening. Even the rank amateur electricians on Centauri Station didn't install a fixture from the top down. I stepped out of the restroom.

"Kai, you have security cams in the restrooms?"

"Brother, no! A man needs his privacy."

That from the owner whose toilets had no stalls. I grabbed a chair from a table. "I'm borrowing a chair."

"Yeah, well you move a table in there, and I ain't serving you. That place reeks."

I pulled the chair in after me. Danny Boy followed. I climbed up, and with my height could easily lift the inoperative fan straight up. I slid it right, and rested it inside the ceiling. I pulled my pocket flashlight out, popped my head into the opening, and probed around with the flashlight's beam. The ductwork was gone, replaced by a few pieces of used decking between the supports. Just enough to carry the weight of a man or two between here and the maintenance access.

I jumped down and moved the chair back against the wall. I trained the light on the sticky floor. A few dried, dark brown drops appeared.

61

"Danny Boy, analyze the surface of this deck right here."

Danny Boy hovered over, dropped to a half meter from the floor, and sent an emerald beam back and forth across the area.

"Standard duranium and steel decking. Surface accretion consisted of 86% urine, 8% fecal—"

"Uh, no! Skip the scatological items. Focus on the brown dried drops. Are they blood?"

"Yes."

"Type and match the DNA."

"The DNA is a 99.98% match for Crewman Lafontaine."

I'd found Lafontaine's escape route. But it was looking a lot more like his murderer's escape route. It would have taken one massive guy to lift Lafontaine up and into the ceiling after overpowering him.

I had my first clue about the killer. There was still some real cop in me after all.

◆◆◆

I sent Danny Boy up and into the maintenance access to scan for traces of Lafontaine's blood or any other DNA between there and Lafontaine's final resting place. Even with as specific a set of instructions as I could manage, I assumed he'd screw it up, find nothing, or both. I considered blocking the restroom off as a crime scene, but a real crime would be to have drunk patrons staggering out of Sato's pissing in the corners of the corridors. Besides, I'd gained all I was going to from the place, including a residual aroma on my shirt.

I returned to my office to begin a second pass through the station personnel records. I fired up the coffeemaker. The time for serious police work had arrived.

I cross-referenced the records until my eyes wept for mercy, but there weren't any connections. Wally walked in carrying a small black plastic bag and cut short my third cursing tirade of the evening.

"Hey Chief. Look what I got a hold of." Today his gloves were amber. The ever-present tan leather bowler covered his head. He sported a matching pair of leather pants. He pulled a bottle of honest-to-God Terran whiskey from the bag with the flair of a magician.

"Wally, what a score!"

He handed me the bottle. The date was thirty years old, the label read Scotland. Knowing how efficiently Centauri Station was resupplied, the bottle had probably been shipped here on the date of manufacture. I frowned. "You need to tell me you didn't steal this."

"Chief, I'm stunned at your lack of faith. Sato had a case ordered. I added one bottle for myself. Legal and paid for."

Now I could drink without guilt, though I had enough practice drinking with guilt that I probably could have forced the liquor down either way. I made a mental note to ask Sato why I only got the bargain basement whiskey when he bought stuff like this. Wally pulled two mugs from beside my dry coffee pot and poured.

"To what do I owe this magnanimous gesture?" I asked as we clinked mugs.

"Friendship. Oh, and I figured you might need a little unwinding after working the station's first murder case in forever."

"Yeah, lucky me." I took a swallow. The burn felt warm and good.

"Progress?"

"Slow." I leaned back in my chair and stared at the ceiling. "You see the station from a different perspective than I do. Any rumors about the killing? Any stories about Lafontaine?"

"Mostly shock, and more than a little fear. Everyone's certain there's a killer on station."

My comm beeped. The ID said it was the station captain. The last time he called was…damn, I couldn't remember. I answered.

"Security."

"Landers?" A barely measured panic permeated his voice. "How close are you to solving that crewman's murder?"

"And good evening to you, Captain. I'm fine. Thanks for asking. The investigation into the Lafontaine murder is still ongoing."

"Well the *Canberra Lance* just docked and all crew members have been denied station shore leave. The *Salvatore Greene's* captain has shouted to the galaxy that one of his crew was murdered here and the *Lance's* captain isn't taking any risks. No shore leave means a big revenue hit for us. Two other ships have just flat-out rerouted. You need to wrap this up double quick before we turn into a ghost station."

"Well, Cap, I was going to drag the investigation out to savor it, but since you insist, I'll get right on it."

"Is that you being a smart-ass?"

"No, this is my natural response to your stellar leadership. Security out." I closed the link.

"You don't get along with a lot of people," Wally observed.

"You noticed?"

"Ever think it might be you?"

"Don't see how it could be," I said.

"Me neither." Wally stood and slipped the bottle back in the bag. "I'll let you go back to winning friends and influencing people. We'll tap this again when you catch the killer."

"The good news there," I said, "is that whiskey tastes better as it ages."

◆◆◆

"Security Lead Landers! You're needed on the lower docking ring."

The loud voice woke me like an air horn from the soundest of sleep. I jerked straight up out of bed and slammed my head on Danny Boy's underside. It was like hitting a steel bulkhead.

"Son of a bitch!"

Danny Boy hovered away from the bed. "Sir, there is a body in Bay Four on the lower docking ring."

A knot slowly rose on my forehead. Another formed in my stomach. "What body?"

"The details are unclear."

For a machine that could tap into the station mainframe, Danny was frequently damn obtuse.

"Good. Bay Four. I'll meet you there. Begin preliminary scans."

Danny Boy hovered off. The clock read 0402. I slipped on yesterday's uniform from the pile on the floor.

For Zero-Dark-Thirty in the morning, there was quite a crowd around Bay Four when I arrived. Anyone off-duty seemed to have risen for the occasion, and it looked like several on duty had managed to wedge a visit into their busy schedule. Best news of all, Doc Brace was already there. Banging my head on Danny Boy would be a pleasure compared to speaking with him this early. Or at all. I sighed and approached the group.

"Make a hole here people," I said.

The crowd parted like pulled taffy until finally the last two blocking my way moved. The cargo bay doors were wide open. Doc Brace stood in the center of the dirty, empty bay. I scanned the far corners and saw nothing.

"Danny told me there was a body here," I said.

"Someone would have to," Brace said. "They'll retire this station before you ever uncover a crime on it. Here's another happy customer of your police protection."

Brace pointed up over his head. Twenty meters up, a limbless, desiccated corpse lay across three wiring conduits. The face stared down at me, skin stretched back in a rictus smile over huge, white teeth, eyes nothing more than dark sockets. Its hair was just gray stubble. Danny Boy hovered nearby, painting the corpse with bright green laser lines.

"Time of death?" I asked.

"Hmm, let me see," Brace said. "It's 0415, so I'd place it at exactly... How the hell can I give you any answer? I can say that the only thing on this station that's been dead longer than that guy is your career."

"Don't you have snake oil and poultices to prep back in the medical bay? I'll send the body over when we get it down."

Brace's face reddened with anger. "Keep an eye on him, Sheriff. Even dead, he's still wily enough to escape your custody."

Brace left. Danny hovered back down from the ceiling.

"Who is he, Danny Boy?"

"Unknown. His DNA does not match a past or present member of the Centauri Station crew."

My heart sank. Another dead visitor. One killing is murder. Two is a pattern. Same missing limbs. Same stuffing of the rest of the body into some out of the way place. It wasn't a copycat, because Body #1 up there had been dismembered long before yesterday's Body #2 in Engineering ever became common knowledge. Common police practice is that three murders classify a perp as a serial killer. I was willing to give this guy the benefit of the doubt and classify him at only two, if it meant I might prevent number three.

I went back to the crowd at the cargo bay doors. Ensign Hansen, the cargo officer, stood there with a nervous look on his boyish face. I always wondered who he pissed off to get assigned here. Looked like he was worried I'd close down ship ops for a while and sink his schedule.

"Hansen, can you get someone to hover a maglift up there and get that body to Doc Brace's?"

"Sure thing, Chief."

I rolled my eyes. It said Security Lead on my office door, for God's sake. How hard could that be?

I scattered the crowd outside the door and sealed it with a code I shared with the ensign. We hadn't used the lower docking ring in forever since the station's low volume of ships never filled the upper ring. The dormant bays had minimum power and no security cams. Sanitation crews didn't even visit, so who knew how long that poor bastard had been literally hanging around up there.

"Danny Boy, go to each of the other cargo bays on this ring. Scan for any corpses, body parts, or blood splatter and then report back to me."

Danny Boy headed down the corridor. I began my usual second guessing of my instructions. They seemed clear but… There were times I wished I could make him repeat my commands back to me so I was sure he understood them.

I had my own avenue to investigate, a little "human intelligence" as the military used to say. Though plenty of people would have said neither word applied to Wally.

◆◆◆

Wally's cargo bay was wide open, the hatch to his ship as well. Having little worth stealing significantly reduced the threat of theft. I stuck my head in the door.

The escape shuttle from Wally's terraforming scout ship was designed to seat four, barely. Wally had spent months alone in this oversized closet, and in spite of, or maybe because of that, he just kept it as his onboard living space. Extra gear and ship castoffs cluttered the place. He'd torn out two of the seats, installed a hammock, and turned one of the walls into an open wardrobe for the odd assortment of clothing he called his personal apparel. Leather was the predominant theme, but in the cloth components, no garish color seemed to go unrepresented. He was the only guy I ever knew, or woman now that I think about it, with multiple sets of gloves. And people say spending months alone in an escape pod can turn you crazy. What fools.

Wally snoozed in the hammock.

"Wally?"

His head lolled right and he opened one eye. "Aren't you the early bird?"

He sat up in the hammock and stretched. All he wore was a tight set of red leather underpants. He didn't have the physique for them. I turned away to keep from being blinded.

"Damn, Wally, put something on. And leather underwear?"

I heard his feet hit the deck as he hopped out of the hammock. "Chief, wearing leather gives you skin on skin. No softer feeling in the world. Don't knock it 'till you try it."

"I'll put it on my bucket list."

Clothing rustled. I turned around and he was dressed, including his stupid bowler hat. He swept some boxes from one of the seats and pointed for me to sit down. I did and he took the other chair.

"What brings you to my *casa famosa*?"

"Another body a few bays down. Been there a while. Also missing limbs. Have you noticed anyone down here acting suspicious?"

"*Anybody* down here would be suspicious. This place is a tomb. Ooh, bad choice of words. Anyhow, I'll go weeks without seeing someone. Was it another crewman on shore leave?"

"Probably." I sighed.

"You'll catch the guy," Wally said. "I know you will."

"Really?" His confidence wasn't remotely contagious.

"Seriously, Chief, you got what it takes." His voice lost some of its fuzzy edge. "I did all the tech maintenance when I was with terraform recon. One thing they did was called sonic strata mapping."

Wally picked up a probe from the corner of the room, about a meter long, with a bulb-like a cattail at the top. He dropped it point first on the deck.

"With this, you squeeze the end and it sends out a sonic pulse. The ship records how the sound wave travels and in seconds we had the geology of the area completely mapped, composition, strata, water tables. Everything.

"That guy's job was like yours. Taking a lot of information and making a big picture from it."

He ran the probe tip across the deck.

"Difference is, all you get to see is this, the surface. You have to dig by hand for every clue, and then you only get to see whatever you hold. You guess about the rest. You even guess where to dig."

"Yeah, it's a wonder I find anything when you look at it that way," I said.

"But you do. I've seen it. When you caught those guys smuggling doped up sawbill mice? That was all police work."

Just after Wally arrived, I'd caught a crew smuggling Tellurian sawbill mice in stasis. The mice are bizarre looking, a real draw in the illegal pet trade. But they are prone to carrying a rare, nasty virus. When a crewman had to be treated for that virus, and I saw stasis fluid on the manifest for no reason, I had Danny Boy search until he found the mice in a bulkhead. Small victory, but the first I'd had since being stationed here. Nice that Wally noticed. The station captain and my superiors never did.

"Well," I said. "If that's true I'm not going to solve it sitting here. If you remember seeing anything suspicious, let me know."

Wally pulled yesterday's bottle of whiskey from a drawer behind him. "One to get the juices flowing?"

"Before 0500?"

"Time is arbitrary on a space station. Could just as easily be 1700, I say."

"We'll wait until the case is solved."

"Deal."

Back in my office, I sent the ship's computer on a massive hunt. I had it pull the crew manifests of every ship that has passed through in the last twelve months. I sent that data to Danny Boy for DNA comparison. Then I pulled the manifests of all those ships at their next port of call and had the names cross-referenced. Four ships showed discrepancies like the *Salvatore Greene*. Three came up a crewman short at their next port call. One came up a crewman over and accounted for one of the missing men, who had apparently been recruited to switch ships. That left two vessels with a man left behind on Centauri Station.

The *Deepwater Gulf* left an engine tech named Ben Garvey. The *Marianna Molina* departed without a bilge scrubber named Sven Bahus.

Danny Boy beeped in on the com.

"There are no bodies, body parts, or blood in any of the other cargo bays," Danny said. "But I have a DNA match for the victim in Bay 4."

I flipped a mental coin. "Ben Garvey."

"That is correct."

It was quite a disappointment that Danny was incapable of being impressed by my seemingly magic intuition. It would have been high-fives all around with Wally.

"Return to the office," I said, and closed the comm link.

The *Marianna Molina* left Bahus behind about a month before Garvey went missing, which was thirty-one days ago. So I expected Bahus' decomposing body was somewhere on board, by now probably skeletal, and my serial killer had three-victim street cred.

The only bright side of this was more data points. I had the computer cross-reference all three missing men, and then all three with every station crewmember who had been on board since the *Marianna Molina's* departure. That gave me another big, fat pile of nothing.

A real nightmare scenario dawned on me. The killer could be acting completely randomly. A random choice of target, location and time would mean I'd never prevent murder number four.

The comm beeped again. Doc Brace this time. The day just kept getting better.

"Security."

"News on the latest unhappy customer of your benevolent protection," Brace said. "Looks like the same killer. The skull has one puncture wound. Limbs sliced through the bone clean and neat. The rest of him is too far gone to tell much else. I'd estimate date of death at—"

"Thirty-one days ago."

Brace paused. Now *that* was the reaction Danny Boy couldn't muster.

"Uh, plus or minus three days, yeah. You working my medical side of the street now?"

"Why not? You barely are."

Brace grumbled. Zinger on target. "Aren't you due a prostate check? Have I mentioned the old fashioned method is the best?"

"The corpse was a crewman named Garvey off a freighter. Keep him on ice as evidence."

I killed the link before I had to endure any more of our upgraded veterinarian. I called up the records of Sven Bahus so I'd have an idea what kind of body I'd come across later.

Bahus was huge. 6'4" and 280 pounds of rippling muscle with a bullet of a shaved head atop a neck just as wide. Good luck getting that body stuffed between some water pipes. He worked ship sanitation and, from his record, he was lucky to get that. The *Marianna Molina's* low standards gave Centauri Station's a run for the money. Bahus boasted felony convictions for assault on a police officer and attempted murder. Psych profile was borderline sociopath, and prison docs were notorious for underdiagnosing to get inmates released. No wonder his captain didn't report him missing. If he was onboard Centauri Station, maybe having him dead wasn't such a bad thing after all.

I started a mental checklist of who on board would be able to take this guy down without getting killed, and without making such a production of it that everyone on deck heard. The list got damn short damn fast. Then an awful revelation hit.

Maybe he wasn't dead.

He was the first one missing. Maybe he wasn't killed, maybe he stayed behind to be the killer. He had the history for it. A voyage scrubbing the bowels of an old freighter might have been enough to flip the nut job switch. He would have been strong enough to kill Lafontaine and hoist him up through the ceiling at Sato's. He'd have no trouble wedging Garvey into the pipes in Bay 4.

I had the computer search for his retinal scan signature on any of the station videos. In Centauri Station style, the memory core was only large enough to keep a three-month backlog. He wasn't on any of them. That meant he had to be living somewhere without surveillance. That left most of the lower docking ring open, and all the maintenance passages. A lot of cubic feet to cover between me and a buzzy, floating robot.

Danny Boy returned.

"Danny Boy, was there any sign anyone was living in any of the cargo bays you inspected?"

"That was not part of the command request."

"I know that. Review the scans of the cargo areas. Look for bedding, clothing…" I hated to say it, but there aren't restrooms around there. "…traces of human bodily waste."

Danny Boy paused and processed. "None of those indicators were found. Only Bay 4 showed any disturbance of what looked like long term dust."

That narrowed it down to the maintenance areas. I pulled up a three-dimensional schematic of the station. Sato's and the lower ring were all on the ship's lower half. There was a lot of traffic around the outer edge passages for regular checks of radiation shielding and the solar panels, but hardly anyone went down the center to the empty comm array bay at the station's tail. An upgrade had moved all the transmission hardware deeper into the better-protected hull. If I was going to hide somewhere, the array area would be the place.

I called the maintenance chief and had him quietly pull back any men he had working in the lower levels. He didn't ask why, but I guessed that with two murders on the station, he didn't need to. When he confirmed the area was clear, I secured the compression doors to the upper levels. If Bahus was down there, he wasn't getting out. Except through me.

I went into the closet and pulled my weapons belt from a hanger on the wall. Greeting only the most suspect of ships had ever warranted me walking the station armed before. The stun gun blinked red and ready. I wanted Bahus alive.

Sidearm at one hip, stun gun on the other, the weapons belt sagged against my hips. The weight I'd been completely accustomed to long ago now seemed so heavy. The whole job was starting to feel that way.

I headed for the office door, Danny Boy in tow. I nearly bowled over Wally on his way in. He looked surprised. The color of the day was red, shirt and gloves both. He gave my weapons belt a long hard look, then patted my stun gun.

"Armed for bear, Chief? Looks like you have a lead."

"I just might. Stay in the upper ring until I get back, just in case. What do you need?"

"Wow. I was coming to tell you I remembered hearing noises from the lower levels a few nights ago, well after maintenance hours. Thought it might matter."

That cinched it. "It might. Stay up here."

◆◆◆

Moments later Danny Boy and I stood in front of the compression door to the lower antenna array. He'd cleared the maintenance passages all the way to here. If Bahus was still alive, he was on the other side of that door.

I drew my stun gun and checked the charge. Nothing. Damn it. Well, let a device sit idle for a few months and it's sure to go bad. I holstered it and drew my revolver instead. Burned by the stun gun, I double-checked that it had six rounds of low impact ammo. Enough to punch through a man's skin, nowhere near enough to then punch through the hull. The revolver was loaded.

I wouldn't have much time. The decompression doors worked loud and slow. Unless Bahus was asleep, when I opened it, I'd lose the element of surprise.

I tapped the code into the door panel. It decompressed with a hiss. Chains clanked against the floor on the other side. Bahus wasn't asleep. I readied my pistol and hit the button. The door slid open.

With the comm gear removed, the empty room looked huge. But it didn't diminish Bahus. The enormous man stood at the far end, stripped down to a just a pair of gray shorts, and white ankle and wrist bands. Every bulging muscle coiled ready to strike. His wide face screwed up in crimson rage. He charged me like a rhino.

First instinct when a freight train of a guy closes on you is to get the hell out of the way. Years of training trumped my instincts. I dropped to one knee, grasped my pistol with both hands and fired twice. The pistol barked and two shots hit Bahus' chest dead center. He didn't even slow. Instinct shouted an "I-told-you-so" to my training.

I ripped three more shots into his midsection and left shoulder with just as much effect. One bullet remained. I held my breath. Bahus closed to a meter away. The stink of his rank sweat filled my nose, the fury that rumbled within him echoed in my gut. I trained the pistol dead between his eyes and fired.

The bullet punctured his forehead with a neat red circle, but the exit wound exploded the back of his head like a ripe melon. But the few grams of bullet couldn't blunt the inertia of three hundred pounds of psycho killer. I flinched left. Bahus' corpse sailed past me and hit the floor with a heavy thud like a slab of beef. I exhaled.

"You have discharged your weapon," Danny Boy said. "Shall I call for assistance?"

I thought that maybe Dumb Bastard might have been a better name for him after all. "No, I think I got this one, Danny." I glanced into Bahus' lair. "Make a Level Three scan of the room for the permanent record."

Danny whizzed in and began painting the place with jade-shaded light. I gave Bahus the once over. He didn't look any smaller dead. And he certainly didn't smell any better. A few months without bathing didn't do him any favors.

I headed into the comm room. At the far end were the chains I heard him kick against when the door decompressed. Four short lengths, each bolted to the wall, each with a remote-release shackle at the end, standard psych ward prison issue. Bahus must have chained his prisoners here before they begged for execution.

In the corner lay a few tools to help get around the maintenance area, wrenches to unbolt panels, crowbars, a door lock override the maintenance techs used when passcodes went haywire. On top lay Bahus' person tool of the slaughterhouse trade, a sonic scraper. The Y-shaped, handheld device generated a high-frequency sonic wave between the tines. Bilge techs like Bahus used it to vibrate buildup from hull interiors, especially in engine rooms, without ever having to scrape a thing. Used properly, it could sear the rust off a heat baffle. Used improperly, it could sever a limb or four off a corpse.

"Danny when you scan the sonic scraper here, go microscopic for trace DNA." That would just be a formality. I knew what three sets the bot would find.

My comm beeped. The station captain. Splendid.

"Security."

"Landers, I'm up in your office looking for an update. Where the hell are you?"

"I went for a spacewalk to clear my head. It's lovely out here. C'mon out. You don't even need a pressure suit."

"You're about to smart-ass yourself out of a job. Any closer to finding that killer?"

I walked back over and stood by Bahus. His pooling blood lapped the toe of my boot. "You could say that."

♦♦♦

The rest of the day was a whirlwind of tagging crime scene files, answering stupid questions from stupid people, and filling out reports. Weapons discharge in the line of duty, multiple murders, suspect termination with extreme prejudice. This whole event rang every bell in the legal system, and each demanded a different explanation to a different person several million miles away. Add in the comm signal delay back and forth to my already low tolerance for explaining myself, and by the evening I was kind of wishing I'd left Bahus sealed in there to starve to death in secret.

But, the end result was cheers all around. No one up the chain of command threatened me with prosecution. Everyone on the station was relieved that the killer had been found, and even more relieved that it hadn't been one of them. Even the station captain smiled, shook my hand and said thanks. Three ships had changed their minds and kept their old flight plans, including a stop at Centauri Station. That probably had something to do with his uncharacteristic good humor.

As the action subsided around 2200 hours, I should have been thrilled and exhausted. But I was neither.

My career hadn't wound up on this spinning pile of scrap metal by accident. I had a habit of making supremely self-destructive decisions. My penchant for personal sabotage was legendary. Maybe I didn't think I deserved success, maybe the cynic in me thought everything positive was too good to be true, and the rest of me made sure it was. I'd brought a dozen cases to near conclusion over the years, only to screw up something at the last minute.

So second-guessing my success at this point would have been a natural response, having tasted success so rarely. But it wasn't winning that stuck my mind in spin cycle. Something didn't fit. Several somethings, in fact.

I fired up the coffee pot, sat down at my desk, pulled up the files from Danny's scans, and began to dig.

◆◆◆

Wally stuck his head and bowler hat into my office about 0100. "Whoa, Chief. Case closed. What are you still doing here?"

"Dotting some I's, crossing some Ts. What are you doing here?"

Wally stepped in. This morning he wore was a leather vest over a solar-flare-orange long sleeve. He flourished the bottled of well-aged whiskey. "I was on my way to your quarters. A deal's a deal, and we need to celebrate."

"I guess we do. Pull up a chair."

I grabbed two mugs and put them on my desk. I sat in the chair beside Wally, between him and the door. Wally poured whiskey in both mugs, started to replace the cap, then ceremoniously set it aside. "Let's keep our options open."

Wally took a swig from his mug. I held mine in my lap.

"You ought to feel good," he said. "This is some serious validation. No one can doubt your police skills anymore."

"No, I look the hero all the way around."

"See, I told you. I always knew it."

"Couple of loose ends I wish I'd tied up before Bahus made me end his life."

"Like?"

"Well, the limbs for one thing. Where the hell are they?"

"Incinerated. Spaced. Tucked away someplace sick. Who knows? Whatever he did to dispose of them, the bodies were probably too big for it."

"So he just left the bodies lying around? He had plenty of time to use the sonic scraper to slice and dice them up."

"Well, I guess you can't figure out a psycho. That's why they're a psycho."

"There also weren't any trophies. Serial killers almost always take trophies from the victims. In fact, there wasn't a trace of any victim anywhere in the comm array room. Odd for a killing zone. And the chains? They didn't make sense."

"Sure looked like they make sense. Gotta bind the victims up."

"But remote unlock shackles? Why bother? Bahus was right there with the victims. A length of wire would do the same thing easier."

Wally shifted in his seat. "He probably had a fixation about them from his time in prison psych wards, had to use them on others the way they were used on him."

"But you know what two things really got me thinking? Danny's DNA scan on the sonic scraper. I got Lafontaine's DNA and Garvey's DNA. But nothing from Bahus. With all the handling he did?"

"Just one of those odd things, I guess."

"Theories have been based on less. Want to hear mine?"

Sweat beaded on Wally's upper lip. "Yeah, sure. I'm up for a campfire story."

"I think someone framed Bahus. With his record, he sure fit the role. Kidnapped him first, chained him in the old comm room. That's why he had those wrist and ankle bands, so the shackles wouldn't damage his skin, so there'd be no physical proof later that he'd been restrained. Once I was on to Bahus, he could be remotely released and fit the bill as the killer."

"Which he would deny, with proof. So much for that theory."

"Unless the arresting officer had to kill him, because someone, an electronics whiz, had discharged the cop's stun gun." I patted my stun gun with my left hand. "Like that."

Wally didn't say a word.

"And finally, no murder weapon."

"He killed them with the sonic scraper."

"No, the two were killed with something powerful and pointy. A lot like the probe you used terraforming."

Wally set his mug on the desk. So did I. He took off his bowler and set it in his lap. My hand slid to rest on my holstered pistol.

"That's coincidental," he said.

"Like you dropping by to check on the progress of the case so often?" I said. "Or you giving me the supposed tip to confirm Bahus was down in the old comm array bay."

"Yeah, coincidental like that."

"Backed up with some interesting evidence." I slid a tablet on the desk over to Wally with my left hand. The picture on it was an x-ray view of a hidden cargo hold, filled with bones. "I sent Danny on a little EVA. Your shuttle decking has a subtle scan dampening field, but it's easy to look in from the outside. Hello trophy room."

All the fear left Wally's face. His eyes narrowed. His gloved hands gripped his bowler tight. "How about I tell you a campfire story?"

I slid my pistol half way out of the holster. "I'm all ears."

"I escaped the terraforming ship accident in the shuttle, but I didn't do it alone. There were three others, with food and water for a week or two at most. Out in the middle of nowhere, it would take months to get to a shipping lane where we might get rescued. We all did the math in our heads. I was the only one who acted."

"You killed them all," I said.

"No, I said I did the math. That still wouldn't leave enough supplies. I overpowered them while they were sleeping, trussed them up and gave them enough to keep them alive. Then I harvested them."

My stomach roiled at the thought.

"Oh don't be so judgmental. It was life or death, and I chose life. And while it's an acquired taste, the flesh of man does grow on you. A few months here and I had to satisfy the craving." He tapped the picture on the screen. "Those aren't trophies. They're soup starter."

He tugged at his leather vest. "Now my wardrobe? They're trophies."

He pulled open the vest. Lafontaine's bird tattoo adorned the inside. The inner, less finished seams were shaped like a man's upper arm.

My right hand itched to pull my pistol and terminate the sick bastard. I fought back my fury and revulsion. "Why the elaborate ruse, the frame job?"

"Because I like you, Chief. I told you before, I saw greatness in you that needed to be discovered. And if I left you the right trail of breadcrumbs, I knew you'd find it."

"You didn't think that some of the breadcrumbs would lead to you."

"Well, yes." Wally laughed. "Even I, your only supporter, underestimated you. I'll assume that you have all your theories on record somewhere."

"All over. There's nowhere you can outrun the law."

"And you're recoding this?"

"Broadcasting it, actually. Say hi to the folks at Fleet Security."

Wally sighed. "And that's why no plan's complete without a backup plan. What story's better than hero cop takes in criminal mastermind? Hero cop *dies* taking in criminal mastermind."

Wally flipped his bowler so the inside faced me. My gut sank like a rock. A mat of plastic explosive lined the interior. A red light glowed at one end. His thumb hovered over a button.

"I designed it for suicide, but I'm willing to share for your greater glory. Congratulations on cracking your last case."

This time my instinct kicked training's ass and took charge. I dove for the side of my desk. Before I got there, the world went white.

◆◆◆

My eyes fluttered open to see the looming face of Doc Brace.

"The face of Satan," I rasped. "I died and went to hell."

"Like I could get that lucky," Brace said.

He shined a light in my eye. I recoiled.

"Well," he said, "you have a concussion, which is amazing having a brain the size of a peanut."

My arms were wrapped in what looked like insulated aluminum foil. I turned my head on the world's stiffest neck. I was in the medical bay. "Your house of horrors looks way worse from the inside."

Brace squeezed my arm. I yelped.

"Does that hurt?" he said.

"Hell, yeah!"

"That's because you have 3rd degree burns. But I saved both your arms. You're welcome. The scars will remind you to be less stupid in the future. Who the hell lets a guy bring a bomb into a police station?"

"The same kind of guy who lets a veterinarian patch him up."

"Lucky for you I specialized in jackass during residency."

It might have been the pain meds, but I swear I saw just a hint of a smile on Brace's ugly face.

"Rest and take the meds I give you, and you'll recover," he said. "I'll be back to check on you later."

I realized this wasn't going to cut it. No way I wanted to spend the rest of my days owing my life to Brace. I resolved to take up active volcano climbing as soon as I got out of that bed.

I didn't want to break my string of self-destructive decisions.

Ω

Fire Season

Fire season would arrive early this year.

At least that was what Sylvia said. She ran the salvaged, partial sensor arrays, monitored the atmosphere, calculated Ariata's irregular orbit. She'd been right seven seasons running. No one wanted her to be right this time.

That prediction fueled Corrine's haste as she hacked at the vines around her. Her makeshift machete, hammered out of the escape shuttle's now useless wings, had grown dull. There would be time enough to sharpen it soon, two months and two days by Sylvia's estimation. Now there was only time to reap.

Even this close to fire season, the jungle still grew faster each day, fueled by the rising polymethane levels the Ariatian flora thrived on. Vines advanced across the jungle floor like a time-lapse movie. In the canopy, flowers from different trees intertwined like twirling dancers and culminated their courtship with the kiss of pistol and stamen. The trees had no time to trust pollination to the vagaries of wind, as Corrine had no time for anything but the harvest.

She hacked her way to the base of a megafruit tree. The wide, iron-like trunk had survived enough fire seasons to stretch over 10 meters high. Thick branches spread out near the crown and eggplant-shaped orange megafruit hung from strands along each branch. She sliced them free with great sweeps of her machete, and stuffed the fallen fruit into the huge sack at her side, a carryall handmade from the orange remnants of an emergency shelter tent, its day-glow tangerine color faded to a rusty red.

Her sack was only three-quarters full, but she dared not search out a second tree. She heaved the bag up onto her shoulder. She'd seen men struggle to carry less, which made the teenager quite happy.

She turned, and froze in surprise. Eight-year-old Bethany stood a few feet away, hair tied back in a loose ponytail just like Corrine's. The tattered legs of her jumpsuit were a few inches too short.

"Bethany! What are you doing out here?"

"I followed you. You were supposed to gather black nuts, but you went in another direction, so I wanted to see."

Corinne grinned at Bethany's idolizing tone and the star-struck look in her eyes.

"You shouldn't follow me," Corinne said in a monotone devoid of admonishment.

She handed Bethany the makeshift scythe. Bethany took it with near-royal reverence.

"Now, fly. We have to get back to camp."

Advancing vines already half-covered the route she'd slashed into the jungle. The last thing she needed was to get lost this far from camp. At the jungle's edge, Bethany raced ahead of her, slashing the air with the scythe, mimicking Corinne cutting down the megafruit.

Corinne adjusted the sack higher on her shoulder. Her steps traced the boundary of a reaped field. Stalks of what passed for a brittle version of wheat lay scattered on the ground, the heads hand harvested. The reapers bent low, engrossed in the task, but still cast furtive skyward glances at the ever more brooding southern sky.

She fell in with several other survivors on their way back to camp. Each carried a makeshift sack of Ariata's bounty, whether wild grown like hers or cultivated like the wheat. She sidled up beside Fenton. The middle-aged man with the graying beard had been a hydroengineer before the accident made farmers of them all. Dirt puffed through the shoddy seams of his patchwork sack with every jostling step.

"Corinne! I was just worrying about you."

She tucked her hair behind one ear. "And for no reason, as usual." She patted his lumpy, dusty bag. "My keen intuition guesses you've got potatoes."

"Or as close as we can get, being light years from Idaho," he said. "And you've gathered?"

Her blue eyes twinkled as she whispered, "Megafruit."

"What? Who sent you out for that? It goes bad in days."

"I sent myself," she said. "I was supposed to help with the black nut harvest, but there were plenty of people there. I thought we needed something sweet to celebrate the start of fire season. We'll have a final-night-outdoors-megafruit-party!"

"Girl," he sighed, "there's no time for that, not with the season starting early." He glanced upward. "Not with that sky."

Corinne bumped shoulders with him and smiled. "C'mon! When did all the fun drain out of you, Fenton?"

"About five minutes after we landed here."

They entered the camp area. No harvestable Ariatian trees meant no wood. No wood meant no shelters. Not that anyone had time to waste on something so temporary. Food trumped all from the first day of growing season.

A hill of dirt now covered their stranded savior shuttle. Another two meters of protection between the ship and fire season made survival possible. Only the stack of the engine exhaust coolers stuck out of the top like a wide chimney. The side main access hatch stood up and open. When they sealed it, they'd insulate that weak point from within.

The shuttle seated fifty, but carried over a hundred when it abandoned the dying transport ship *Mercury*. A meteor shower mortally wounded all three ships in the convoy, but no one knew if any other escape craft made it to Ariata. It was a near miracle that the overloaded shuttle had made a survivable landing.

That miracle's creator stood outside the shuttle's hatch. Roland had been just a comm tech on the *Mercury*, but a certified civilian pilot, certified enough to get their limping shuttle down on flat ground. That feat was enough to make him leader, and his pragmatic planning had kept him there ever since.

The gray dust of the Ariatian soil coated the edges of his fading flight jacket. A gust of wind blew his long, dark hair back from his face. He hadn't cut it since the growing season started, hadn't seemed to have done much of anything except manage the planting, the cultivation and now the harvest. Ariata's flora had adapted to its four month growing season with exponential growth rates. Still, every crash survivor spent every minute of daylight in the communal pursuit of a bountiful, life-saving harvest.

"Fenton," he said. "How's the southern harvest coming?"

"The field's almost bare. The last of the crew is on their way."

At the valley's end, the sky had turned a reddish purple as the polymethane concentration hit dangerous levels. On the ridgeline behind the camp, a geyser burped another mass of complex hydrocarbons into the atmosphere. Growing season ended as Ariata

82

passed closest to the sun. The surge in gravitational pull heated the core, and the tectonic shifts opened subterranean gas pockets.

Roland looked over at Corinne. He frowned.

"That sack doesn't look like it's full of nuts."

"Something better!" Corinne smiled. "Megafruit!"

Roland's eyes flashed with anger. "We don't need megafruit, Corinne. We need food we can store. That's why you were assigned where you were. If everyone doesn't do their part—"

An aurora flashed to life across the southern sky. The wispy, blue band rolled toward them. In its wake, bolts of magenta lightning ripped from cloud to ground. Thunder followed, so deep and resonant that the ground trembled.

A scream rose up from the scattered survivors across the valley. They broke into a sprint for the protection of the buried shuttle. Sylvia came running from the shuttle to Roland's side. The chubby little woman hadn't lost an ounce since their stranding, and the short dash left her out of breath and sweating.

"That's the first of many," she said. "There's a storm of solar flares coming like nothing we've ever seen. Lightning charges will be off the chart, probably 300 kiloamps and over a billion volts per strike."

More than enough to ignite the polymethane and start fire season's lengthy atmospheric conflagration, a firestorm incinerating everything on the surface save the stoutest megafuit trees.

As Ariata sheared back away from the sun, the fires would stop. The boiling sea would cool. Ashes would enrich the sterilized soil. After a week of rainfall, buds would burst through the cinders, and life would return.

The only humans to see it would be the ones safe within the buried shuttle.

"What's the head count?" Roland asked Sylvia.

"Seventy-nine in the hull."

Corinne spun the math. That left seventeen outside, including herself and Fenton. She looked into the shuttle. Bethany waved from inside. Corinne exhaled in relief.

"Auxiliary power unit up?" Roland said.

"Stan pulled the last igniter from the main engines to fix it, but it's ready," Sylvia said.

Roland surveyed the people rushing for the shuttle and grimaced. "Sylv, get everyone inside. Pack what they've gathered into the pit and get an accurate count. I've got a bad feeling we didn't make quota." He turned to Corinne. "You and I will talk later. Get in there."

Corrine jogged with Fenton and Sylvia back into the shuttle. The ship's shadowy interior had been stripped down to the inner walls. Everything not bolted down, and most of the things that had been, was stripped away, left outside, and lost during the first fire season. Rows and columns of woven-vine hammocks now filled the interior, strung head to toe and nearly side to side. People stood in the shadows between the makeshift beds, engrossed in worried conversations.

Rudimentary engineering controls and an even more rudimentary water recycling system took up a section of the stern. Stan stood there, coated in sweat and dirt, checking readouts and waiting for the last possible second before bringing the fuel-sucking reactor, lights and life support on line.

Sylvia banged a metal rod against the hull rapid fire. The crowd went still.

"Hit your bunks everyone!" Sylvia ordered. "We need a headcount. Confirm your fire season sibling is here and healthy."

Everyone crawled into their assigned bunk. Hands reached out and touched other's hands as the fire season buddy system began.

Corrine dropped her sack by the open hatch in the floor. A shallow cave-basement ran beneath the ship, hewn by the survivors in a painstaking process that pit hand tools against the basalt-like rock two feet below the valley's ashy surface. Last season, the storage area had been full up to the hatch. Corrine peered over the edge. This season she saw plenty of room. Bethany skipped up to Corrine's side.

"Corrine," Bethany said. "We're fire season siblings. I traded with Maria."

Corrine smiled. Maria was a whiny old thing, always telling her what to do. Bethany would work out much better.

"Then we need to watch out for each other, right?" Corrine said.

"All season long."

84

Corinne shooed Bethany to her bunk. A few stragglers came through the hatch. Sylvia began a headcount. Thunder boomed again in the distance.

Outside, Roland ducked his head against a dusty blast of wind. He retreated to just outside the hatch. Sylvia returned to the doorway and scowled at Corrine.

"Get to your bunk, Corinne." She turned to Roland. "Ninety-two. All accounted for."

"Food?"

"We planned on more."

Roland shook his head, and looked at the ground.

From the jungle's edge, a young woman staggered toward the camp. Her tattered clothes hung in shreds. Dirt caked her legs from her knees to her bare feet. At the sight of the buried shuttle, her face filled with relief. She shuffled forward in a limping jog.

Roland grabbed the metal pole Sylvia had left by the hatch threshold. He squared himself to block the entrance. Sylvia and Corinne watched from inside the shuttle. When the woman was just meters away, Roland lowered the pole in her direction. She stopped. She swayed a bit on her feet.

"Who are you?" he said.

Corinne wondered what difference it made. She was human! They hadn't seen another human since the catastrophe, had assumed they were the only survivors to make it to Ariata, or perhaps the only ones to survive the first fire season.

"Karen Pinkava," she said. Her creaky voice sounded desert dry. "I was on the *Cassandra*. Thank God, I found you. The storms are coming. I was afraid I'd die out here."

"Where have you been for seven seasons?"

"I survived with two others in an escape pod. We found a cave by the sea, lived mostly on seaweed. A week ago, I came back from gathering food and the cave had collapsed, with both of them inside. I just started walking, hoping to find someone, or someplace safe before the storm came. You saved me just in time!"

She took a step forward. Roland stopped her with the tip of the pole. "No, I haven't."

"What do you mean?" Corinne blurted out. "We have to help her."

Sylvia looked at Corinne with fury on her eyes. "With what? You saw the storeroom isn't full, like your spoiling megafruit was any help there. We'll be lucky to get everyone through the fire season alive as it is."

"We don't have any room," Roland told the woman. "Every space is filled with a bunk, and every bunk is filled. Life support is pushed to filter the air and water for that many people as it is."

"She's a human being," Corinne pleaded. "We'll find a way."

"I missed the part where anyone asked you," Sylvia said.

"Corinne, what's happening?"

Bethany had crept up to her side. She squinted in the sunlight. Corinne put an arm around the girl's shoulder.

"These two are just planning a murder," Corinne said.

"You two get back to your bunks, now!" Sylvia commanded.

The sky had become one roiling cloud. A kilometer into the jungle, a new polymethane vent burst the surface of the earth with a roar. Cloud-to-cloud lightning rippled overhead and backlit the sky in bloody red.

"I don't know you," Roland told the woman. "We barely have enough to get us through fire season. We take care of our own. I'm sorry."

Corinne dashed through the doorway, past Roland to Karen's side. She wrapped her arm around the woman's thin waist. Karen collapsed against Corrine. Corinne struggled to keep her upright.

"Fine," Corrine said, chin raised in defiance. "Leave her out here and you leave me here. What threat could she be? She can barely stand? She needs our help."

"Damn it," Roland said. "We have no help to give. Who will you ask to give up their rations for a stranger?"

By now a crowd of the curious had gathered behind Sylvia. Heads jostled each other for a peek at the unfolding event. In the jungle, another polymethane vent erupted with a bang. The crowd flinched.

Corinne cinched the limp woman tighter. She spoke past Roland, directly to the faces that seemed to float in the shuttle interior's darkness.

"We're light years from home, but we are still human beings!" she shouted.

86

She squinted and angled her head into a sudden gust of wind. The breeze blew itself out and left the side of her face caked in dark ash.

"This woman is also a human being. We have to do whatever it takes to help her! If not, what have we become?"

"Survivors," Sylvia said. "That's what we've become."

A murmur of assent rippled through the faces behind her.

"And you're pretty quick to give away our food," one man said. "Considering you weren't even out there picking with us today."

A few voices sounded off in approval. Corrine figured Maria had to be one of them. Something beeped inside the shuttle. Sylvia vanished then reappeared, face flushed.

"We need to seal this hatch! Polymethane saturation had crossed the threshold level."

The people inside scampered for their bunks. Roland stepped inside the shuttle threshold.

"Come in alone, Corrine," he said. "Or stay out there and prove how little you care about your people. But you make the decision now."

Corinne could see in his face that he was bluffing. He wouldn't leave her out here. Lightning flashed over the ridge behind the shuttle. The thunder rumbled like a band of kettle drums. Corinne swept a few stray hairs behind her ear.

"You have to take us both," she declared.

"Your choice," Roland said.

He pulled the hatch shut. The double locks clicked on the other side.

Corinne's jaw dropped. He couldn't have… The rest of them wouldn't let him…

Movement on top of the buried shuttle caught her eye. Her heart skipped a beat. Bethany came skidding down the dusty hillside on her butt. At the bottom she popped to her feet with a smile.

"Bethany! What the hell are you doing out here?"

"We're fire season siblings." Her voice brimmed with misspent pride. "You said we watch out for each other, all season long."

"Goddammit!" Karen shouted.

She burst from Corinne's embrace with such force it sent Corinne flying backwards.

"Kid, for a moment I thought you were about to save the day," Karen said. "But that guy in there must really hate your guts."

Karen raised her fingers to her lips and let loose a piercing whistle toward the jungle.

Six ragged, muscular men burst from the jungle's edge at a run. They wore mismatched remnants of Interstellar Defense Force uniforms. The larger transports had each carried a detachment of them. All of the men were armed with a variety of lethal-looking homemade spears and battle-axes.

"Corrie?" Bethany said in a voice two octaves too high.

Bethany ran up and clamped her arms around Corinne's leg. Her little body shivered against Corrine's thigh. The men gathered around Karen.

"That didn't work out worth a shit," Karen said.

"We should have just rushed the place when we found it," one soldier said.

"I didn't know if this was the storage cache," Karen said. "We could have lost the element of surprise and had nothing."

"Which is where we are anyhow," the soldier said.

"Put a lid on it, Corporal," Karen said. The soldier straightened up. "We aren't done yet. I want that hatch off the hinges. Now."

"You can't do that!" Corinne said. "When the fires start, everyone in there will die!"

"It didn't come to that with last season's group," Karen said.

The soldiers moved for the hatch. Corinne rushed up behind the closest one and tried to wrench away his weapon. It was like wrestling with a statue. The soldier yanked it from her grip, and then walloped her across the cheek with the butt of the shaft. Stars exploded in her head. She careened backwards and hit the ground hard.

"Corrie!" Bethany shrieked, and ran to her side.

The six men went to work on the hatch. Weapons banged and scraped against the door and hinges. One picked up a rock the size of his head and began to bash the hull. Karen stood beside them. She raised a hand and they stopped.

"This is Commander Karen Pinkava of the Interstellar Defense Force," she shouted at the hatch. "I've got six soldiers out here with me who need quarters from the storm. The choice you have is let us in, or we let ourselves in through a damaged hatch, and all of you get to enjoy the change of seasons with us."

"If there wasn't food for one extra, there won't be food for seven," Corinne said.

Karen bent closer to Corinne and whispered, "That's why seven farmers will have to spend the night out here. Then again, maybe fourteen, we tend to eat a lot."

Karen stood next to the hatch and listened. No one answered her demands. Corrine knew Roland wouldn't. He wouldn't open the hatch to someone he couldn't trust, wouldn't expose the others. The *Mercury* survivors took care of their own.

And weren't they doing a piss-poor job of that right now? Stan hadn't fired up the APU. Ninety people were sitting in absolute darkness in a buried metal box, with no life support. What was Roland waiting for?

Suddenly, she knew. They were taking care of their own.

Karen ordered the soldiers back to work. The six assaulted the hatch and hull with a vengeance. The clang of metal-on-metal echoed in the valley.

"Bethany," Corinne whispered, "how did you get out here?"

"The APU exhaust vent. I opened up the service panel and climbed up the rungs."

Which meant she left the service panel in the shuttle open. Roland had put two and two together as soon as he knew Bethany was missing. He'd ordered the APU kept offline until the last minute, to give Bethany and her a way back in. If they could make it in time.

Another ripple aurora rolled across the purple sky, this one wider and thicker than the last. A sheet of lightning arced to the ground in its wake. Pockets of concentrated polymethane burst along its path to the ground. Booms of thunder cracked like cannon shots across the valley.

Karen shouted orders to hurry as the soldiers pounded the hatch. Corinne put her mouth to Bethany's ear.

"While they aren't looking," Corinne said, "run up there as fast as you can and get back down that APU vent."

"What about you?"

"I'll be right behind you. Go!"

Bethany jumped to her feet and scrambled up the ashy hill that entombed the shuttle. Corinne stood up and her head felt like it made a complete revolution on her neck. She wobbled, and then scrambled after Bethany.

"Hey!" the corporal shouted. "Where are they going?"

"Get them!" Karen shouted.

Corinne dared not look back, not waste one delaying movement. She stared straight up at Bethany's back as she clawed her way up the loose earth. Corinne climbed behind her, spitting dust and deflecting pebbles from the girls flailing shoes. Behind her snorted the labored breaths of a pursuing soldier. They grew louder with each step.

Bethany hit the top, stood, and sprinted. Corinne rose to follow.

A hand snatched her ankle. She fell on her side and looked down. The corporal looked up at her with a malicious grin on his filthy face. A crude sword hung at his waist.

She reared back with her free foot and kicked him across the face, once, twice. His grip slipped. She pulled her ankle free.

The polymethane-saturated air filled her lungs like syrup. Sweat covered her face. She took a deep, heaving breath and scrambled up to the top of the buried shuttle.

At the far end, Bethany had thrown the bolt and opened the access door to the vent stack. She made a windmill motion with her arm. "C'mon, Corrie!" The thickening air muffled her voice. The atmosphere teetered at ignition.

Corrine ran. She knew the corporal would be on her again in an instant.

"Go, Bethany! I'm right behind you!"

Bethany entered the vent stack, and climbed down the metal rungs and out of sight. A gust of wind blew the door closed. The bolt that secured it rattled in its guide.

A new wave of dread swept over Corrine. That bolt wouldn't lock anyone on the outside out. The soldier would be two steps behind her, follow her down the vent, slash his way to the hatch, and the show would be over.

"You're going to pay for kicking me, little bitch," the corporal yelled from the top of the mound. He came at her at a dead run.

She scooped up a big rock from the dirt mid-stride. She reached the access door and threw the bolt to secure it. She raised the rock over her head and bashed the end of the bolt. On the second strike, it bent down into a L.

She whirled just as the corporal reached for her throat. She brought the rock around and crashed it into his temple. He spun, dropped and hit the dirt.

Behind her, the APU roared to life. Hot air blasted from the vent stack and her back went warm.

All around the valley, a cascade of lightning strikes peppered the ground. Great balls of purple fire billowed to life, grew, and joined. A searing shockwave rolled out across the valley. It roared through the jungle, and even the megafruit tree swayed as it passed. It rolled over the shuttle, swept the corporal down the side and drove Corinne to her knees. Her skin singed and she smelt her hair burn.

Then came the fire. A great wall of purple flame blossomed forward as the chain reaction of the burning polymethane took hold. Acres of jungle withered ahead of the fireball's advance. It rolled over the harvested fields to the camp's edge.

Corinne closed her eyes and thought of Bethany, safe in the shuttle, with one less mouth to feed.

"We take care of our own," she whispered

Ω

Enjoyed the stories?

Let everyone know. Your online reviews do more to spur sales than anything else.

About Author Russell James

Russell R. James was raised on Long Island, New York and spent too much time watching *Chiller*, *Kolchak: The Night Stalker*, and *Dark Shadows*, despite his parents' warnings. Bookshelves full of Stephen King and Edgar Allan Poe didn't make things better. He graduated from Cornell University and the University of Central Florida.

After a tour flying helicopters with the U.S. Army, he now spins twisted tales best read in daylight. He has written the paranormal thrillers *Dark Inspiration*, *Sacrifice*, *Black Magic*, *Dark Vengeance, Dreamwalker,* and *Q Island*, the novella *Blood Red Roses,* as well as the collections *Tales from Beyond, Outer Rim, Forever Out of Time,* and *Deeper into Darkness*.

His wife reads what he writes, rolls her eyes, and says "There is something seriously wrong with you."

Visit his website at http://www.russellrjames.com/ and read some free short stories. Follow on Twitter @RRJames14 or come say hello on Facebook.

Outer Rim

Made in the USA
Columbia, SC
10 April 2023

14750921R00055